WITHDRAWN

SKETCHES.

PREFACE.

A SERIES of designs — suggested, I think, by Hogarth's familiar cartoons of the Industrious and Idle Apprentices — I remember as among the earliest efforts at moral teaching in California. They represented the respective careers of The Honest and Dissolute Miners : the one, as I recall him, retrograding through successive planes of dirt, drunkenness, disease, and death ; the other advancing by corresponding stages to affluence and a white shirt. Whatever may have been the artistic defects of these drawings, the moral at least was obvious and distinct. That it failed, however, — as it did, — to produce the desired reform in mining morality may have been owing to the fact that the average miner refused to recognize himself in either of these positive characters ; and that even he who might have sat for the model of the Dissolute Miner was perhaps dimly conscious of some limitations and circumstances which partly relieved him from responsibility. "Yer see," remarked such a critic to the writer, in the untranslatable poetry of his class, "it ain't no square game. They 've just put up the keerds on that chap from the start."

With this lamentable example before me, I trust that in the following sketches I have abstained from any positive moral. I might have painted my villains of the blackest dye, — so black, indeed, that the originals thereof would have contemplated them with the glow of comparative virtue. I might have made it impossible for them to have performed a virtuous or generous action, and have thus avoided that moral confusion which is apt to arise in the contemplation of mixed motives and qualities. But I should have burdened myself with the responsibility of their creation, which, as a humble writer of romance and entitled to no particular reverence, I did not care to do.

I fear I cannot claim, therefore, any higher motive than to illustrate an era of which Californian history has preserved the incidents more often than the character of the actors, — an era which the panegyrist was too often content to bridge over with a general compliment to its survivors, — an era still so recent that in attempting to revive its poetry, I am conscious also of awakening the more prosaic recollections of these same survivors, — and yet an era replete with a certain heroic Greek poetry, of which perhaps none were more unconscious than the heroes themselves. And I shall be quite content to have collected here merely the materials for the Iliad that is yet to be sung.

San Francisco, December 24, 1869.

CONTENTS.

SKETCHES

STORIES.

BOHEMIAN PAPERS.

THE LUCK OF ROARING CAMP.

THERE was commotion in Roaring Camp. It could not have been a fight, for in 1850 that was not novel enough to have called together the entire settlement. The ditches and claims were not only deserted, but " Tuttle's grocery " had contributed its gamblers, who, it will be remembered, calmly continued their game the day that French Pete and Kanaka Joe shot each other to death over the bar in the front room. The whole camp was collected before a rude cabin on the outer edge of the clearing. Conversation was carried on in a low tone, but the name of a woman was frequently repeated. It was a name familiar enough in the camp, — " Cherokee Sal."

Perhaps the less said of her the better. She was a coarse, and, it is to be feared, a very sinful woman. But at that time she was the only woman in Roaring Camp, and was just then lying in sore extremity, when she most needed the ministration of her own sex. Dissolute, abandoned, and irreclaimable, she was yet suffering a martyrdom hard enough to bear even when veiled by

1   A

sympathizing womanhood, but now terrible in
her loneliness. The primal curse had come to
her in that original isolation which must have
made the punishment of the first transgression
so dreadful. It was, perhaps, part of the expia-
tion of her sin, that, at a moment when she most
lacked her sex's intuitive tenderness and care, she
met only the half-contemptuous faces of her masculine associates. Yet a few of the spectators
were, I think, touched by her sufferings. Sandy
Tipton thought it was "rough on Sal," and, in the
contemplation of her condition, for a moment rose
superior to the fact that he had an ace and two
bowers in his sleeve.

It will be seen, also, that the situation was novel.
Deaths were by no means uncommon in Roaring
Camp, but a birth was a new thing. People had
been dismissed the camp effectively, finally, and
with no possibility of return ; but this was the first
time that anybody had been introduced *ab initio*.
Hence the excitement.

"You go in there, Stumpy," said a prominent
citizen known as " Kentuck," addressing one of
the loungers. " Go in there, and see what you kin
do. You've had experience in them things."

Perhaps there was a fitness in the selection.
Stumpy, in other climes, had been the putative
head of two families ; in fact, it was owing to some
legal informality in these proceedings that Roaring

Camp — a city of refuge — was indebted to his
company. The crowd approved the choice, and
Stumpy was wise enough to bow to the majority.
The door closed on the extempore surgeon and
midwife, and Roaring Camp sat down outside,
smoked its pipe, and awaited the issue.

The assemblage numbered about a hundred men.
One or two of these were actual fugitives from
justice, some were criminal, and all were reckless.
Physically, they exhibited no indication of their
past lives and character. The greatest scamp had
a Raphael face, with a profusion of blond hair ;
Oakhurst, a gambler, had the melancholy air and
intellectual abstraction of a Hamlet ; the coolest
and most courageous man was scarcely over five
feet in height, with a soft voice and an embarrassed,
timid manner. The term "roughs" applied to
them was a distinction rather than a definition.
Perhaps in the minor details of fingers, toes, ears,
etc., the camp may have been deficient, but these
slight omissions did not detract from their aggregate force. The strongest man had but three
fingers on his right hand ; the best shot had but
one eye.

Such was the physical aspect of the men that
were dispersed around the cabin. The camp lay
in a triangular valley, between two hills and a
river. The only outlet was a steep trail over the
summit of a hill that faced the cabin, now illumi-

nated by the rising moon. The suffering woman might have seen it from the rude bunk whereon she lay, — seen it winding like a silver thread until it was lost in the stars above.

A fire of withered pine-boughs added sociability to the gathering. By degrees the natural levity of Roaring Camp returned. Bets were freely offered and taken regarding the result. Three to five that "Sal would get through with it"; even, that the child would survive; side bets as to the sex and complexion of the coming stranger. In the midst of an excited discussion an exclamation came from those nearest the door, and the camp stopped to listen. Above the swaying and moaning of the pines, the swift rush of the river, and the crackling of the fire, rose a sharp, querulous cry, — a cry unlike anything heard before in the camp. The pines stopped moaning, the river ceased to rush, and the fire to crackle. It seemed as if Nature had stopped to listen too.

The camp rose to its feet as one man! It was proposed to explode a barrel of gunpowder, but, in consideration of the situation of the mother, better counsels prevailed, and only a few revolvers were discharged; for, whether owing to the rude surgery of the camp, or some other reason, Cherokee Sal was sinking fast. Within an hour she had climbed, as it were, that rugged road that led to the stars, and so passed out of Roaring Camp, its sin and shame forever. I do not think that the announcement disturbed them much, except in speculation as to the fate of the child. "Can he live now?" was asked of Stumpy. The answer was doubtful. The only other being of Cherokee Sal's sex and maternal condition in the settlement was an ass. There was some conjecture as to fitness, but the experiment was tried. It was less problematical than the ancient treatment of Romulus and Remus, and apparently as successful.

When these details were completed, which exhausted another hour, the door was opened, and the anxious crowd of men who had already formed themselves into a queue, entered in single file. Beside the low bunk or shelf, on which the figure of the mother was starkly outlined below the blankets stood a pine table. On this a candle-box was placed, and within it, swathed in staring red flannel, lay the last arrival at Roaring Camp. Beside the candle-box was placed a hat. Its use was soon indicated. "Gentlemen," said Stumpy, with a singular mixture of authority and *ex officio* complacency, — " Gentlemen will please pass in at the front door, round the table, and out at the back door. Them as wishes to contribute anything toward the orphan will find a hat handy." The first man entered with his hat on; he uncovered, however, as he looked about him, and so, unconsciously, set an example to the next. In such communities good and bad actions are catching. As the procession filed in, comments were audible, — criticisms addressed, perhaps, rather to Stumpy, in the character of showman, — " Is that him ? " " mighty small specimen " ; " has n't mor'n got the color " ; " ain't bigger nor a derringer."   The contributions were as characteristic : A silver tobacco-box ; a doubloon ; a navy revolver, silver mounted ; a gold specimen ; a very beautifully embroidered lady's handkerchief (from Oakhurst the gambler) ; a diamond breastpin ; a diamond ring (suggested by the pin, with the remark from the giver that he " saw that pin and went two diamonds better ") ; a slung shot ; a Bible (contributor not detected) ; a golden spur ; a silver teaspoon (the initials, I regret to say, were not the giver's) ; a pair of surgeon's shears ; a lancet ; a Bank of England note for £ 5 ; and about $ 200 in loose gold and silver coin. During these proceedings Stumpy maintained a silence as impassive as the dead on his left, a gravity as inscrutable as that of the newly born on his right.   Only one incident occurred to break the monotony of the curious procession. As Kentuck bent over the candle-box half curiously, the child turned, and, in a spasm of pain, caught at his groping finger, and held it fast for a moment. Kentuck looked foolish and embarrassed.   Something like a blush tried to assert itself in his weather-beaten cheek. " The d—d little cuss ! "

he said, as he extricated his finger, with, perhaps, more tenderness and care than he might have been deemed capable of showing. He held that finger a little apart from its fellows as he went out, and examined it curiously. The examination provoked the same original remark in regard to the child. In fact, he seemed to enjoy repeating it. "He rastled with my finger," he remarked to Tipton, holding up the member, "the d—d little cuss!"

It was four o'clock before the camp sought repose. A light burnt in the cabin where the watchers sat, for Stumpy did not go to bed that night. Nor did Kentuck. He drank quite freely, and related with great gusto his experience, invariably ending with his characteristic condemnation of the new-comer. It seemed to relieve him of any unjust implication of sentiment, and Kentuck had the weaknesses of the nobler sex. When everybody else had gone to bed, he walked down to the river, and whistled reflectingly. Then he walked up the gulch, past the cabin, still whistling with demonstrative unconcern. At a large red-wood tree he paused and retraced his steps, and again passed the cabin. Half-way down to the river's bank he again paused, and then returned and knocked at the door. It was opened by Stumpy. "How goes it?" said Kentuck, looking past Stumpy toward the candle-box. "All serene," replied Stumpy. "Anything up?" "Nothing."

There was a pause — an embarrassing one —
Stumpy still holding the door. Then Kentuck
had recourse to his finger, which he held up to
Stumpy. " Rastled with it, — the d—d little cuss,"
he said, and retired.

The next day Cherokee Sal had such rude se-
pulture as Roaring Camp afforded. After her
body had been committed to the hillside, there
was a formal meeting of the camp to discuss what
should be done with her infant. A resolution to
adopt it was unanimous and enthusiastic. But an
animated discussion in regard to the manner and
feasibility of providing for its wants at once sprung
up. It was remarkable that the argument partook
of none of those fierce personalities with which
discussions were usually conducted at Roaring
Camp. Tipton proposed that they should send the
child to Red Dog, — a distance of forty miles, —
where female attention could be procured. But
the unlucky suggestion met with fierce and unanimous opposition. It was evident that no plan
which entailed parting from their new acquisition
would for a moment be entertained. " Besides,"
said Tom Ryder, " them fellows at Red Dog would
swap it, and ring in somebody else on us." A dis-
belief in the honesty of other camps prevailed at
Roaring Camp as in other places.

The introduction of a female nurse in the camp
also met with objection. It was argued that no

decent woman could be prevailed to accept Roaring Camp as her home, and the speaker urged that "they did n't want any more of the other kind." This unkind allusion to the defunct mother, harsh as it may seem, was the first spasm of propriety, — the first symptom of the camp's regeneration. Stumpy advanced nothing. Perhaps he felt a certain delicacy in interfering with the selection of a possible successor in office. But when questioned, he averred stoutly that he and " Jinny " — the mammal before alluded to — could manage to rear the child. There was something original, independent, and heroic about the plan that pleased the camp. Stumpy was retained. Certain articles were sent for to Sacramento. " Mind," said the treasurer, as he pressed a bag of gold-dust into the expressman's hand, " the best that can be got, — lace, you know, and filigree-work and frills, — d—m the cost ! "

Strange to say, the child thrived. Perhaps the invigorating climate of the mountain camp was compensation for material deficiencies. Nature took the foundling to her broader breast. In that rare atmosphere of the Sierra foot-hills, — that air pungent with balsamic odor, that ethereal cordial at once bracing and exhilarating, — he may have found food and nourishment, or a subtle chemistry that transmuted asses' milk to lime and phosphorus. Stumpy inclined to the belief that it was the

1 *

latter and good nursing. "Me and that ass," he
would say, "has been father and mother to him!
Don't you," he would add, apostrophizing the helpless bundle before him, "never go back on us."

By the time he was a month old, the necessity
of giving him a name became apparent. He had
generally been known as "the Kid," "Stumpy's
boy," "the Cayote" (an allusion to his vocal
powers), and even by Kentuck's endearing di-
minutive of "the d—d little cuss." But these
were felt to be vague and unsatisfactory, and were
at last dismissed under another influence. Gamblers and adventurers are generally superstitious,
and Oakhurst one day declared that the baby had
brought "the luck" to Roaring Camp. It was
certain that of late they had been successful.
"Luck" was the name agreed upon, with the pre-
fix of Tommy for greater convenience. No allusion was made to the mother, and the father was
unknown. "It's better," said the philosophical
Oakhurst, "to take a fresh deal all round. Call
him Luck, and start him fair." A day was accordingly set apart for the christening. What was
meant by this ceremony the reader may imagine,
who has already gathered some idea of the reckless irreverence of Roaring Camp. The master of
ceremonies was one "Boston," a noted wag, and
the occasion seemed to promise the greatest face-
tiousness. This ingenious satirist had spent two

days in preparing a burlesque of the church service, with pointed local allusions. The choir was properly trained, and Sandy Tipton was to stand godfather. But after the procession had marched to the grove with music and banners, and the child had been deposited before a mock altar, Stumpy stepped before the expectant crowd. " It ain't my style to spoil fun, boys," said the little man, stoutly, eying the faces around him, " but it strikes me that this thing ain't exactly on the squar. It 's playing it pretty low down on this yer baby to ring in fun on him that he ain't going to understand. And ef there 's going to be any godfathers round, I 'd like to see who 's got any better rights than me." A silence followed Stumpy's speech. To the credit of all humorists be it said, that the first man to acknowledge its justice was the satirist, thus stopped of his fun. " But," said Stumpy, quickly, following up his advantage, " we 're here for a christening, and we 'll have it. I proclaim you Thomas Luck, according to the laws of the United States and the State of California, so help me God." It was the first time that the name of the Deity had been uttered otherwise than profanely in the camp. The form of christening was perhaps even more ludicrous than the satirist had conceived; but, strangely enough, nobody saw it and nobody laughed. " Tommy " was christened as seriously as he would have been under a Chris-

tian roof, and cried and was comforted in as orthodox fashion.

And so the work of regeneration began in Roaring Camp. Almost imperceptibly a change came
over the settlement. The cabin assigned to "Tommy Luck" — or "The Luck," as he was more
frequently called — first showed signs of improvement. It was kept scrupulously clean and whitewashed. Then it was boarded, clothed, and papered.
The rosewood cradle — packed eighty miles by
mule — had, in Stumpy's way of putting it, "sorter
killed the rest of the furniture." So the rehabili-
tation of the cabin became a necessity. The men
who were in the habit of lounging in at Stumpy's
to see "how The Luck got on" seemed to appreciate the change, and, in self-defence, the rival es-
tablishment of "Tuttle's grocery" bestirred itself,
and imported a carpet and mirrors. The reflections
of the latter on the appearance of Roaring Camp
tended to produce stricter habits of personal cleanliness. Again, Stumpy imposed a kind of quaran-
tine upon those who aspired to the honor and
privilege of holding "The Luck." It was a cruel
mortification to Kentuck — who, in the careless-
ness of a large nature and the habits of frontier
life, had begun to regard all garments as a second
cuticle, which, like a snake's, only sloughed off
through decay — to be debarred this privilege
from certain prudential reasons. Yet such was the

subtle influence of innovation that he thereafter
appeared regularly every afternoon in a clean shirt,
and face still shining from his ablutions.   Nor
were moral and social sanitary laws neglected.
" Tommy," who was supposed to spend his whole
existence in a persistent attempt to repose, must
not be disturbed by noise.   The shouting and yell-
ing which had gained the camp its infelicitous
title were not permitted within hearing distance
of Stumpy's.   The men conversed in whispers, or
smoked with Indian gravity.   Profanity was tacitly
given up in these sacred precincts, and throughout
the camp a popular form of expletive, known as
" D—n the luck ! " and " Curse the luck ! " was
abandoned, as having a new personal bearing.   Vocal music was not interdicted, being supposed to
have a soothing, tranquillizing quality, and one
song, sung by " Man-o'-War Jack," an English
sailor, from her Majesty's Australian colonies,
was quite popular as a lullaby.   It was a lugu-
brious recital of the exploits of " the Arethusa,
Seventy-four," in a muffled minor, ending with a
prolonged dying fall at the burden of each verse,
" On b-o-o-o-ard of the Arethusa."   It was a fine
sight to see Jack holding The Luck, rocking from
side to side as if with the motion of a ship, and
crooning forth this naval ditty.   Either through
the peculiar rocking of Jack or the length of his
song, — it contained ninety stanzas, and was con-

tinued with conscientious deliberation to the bitter end, — the lullaby generally had the desired effect. At such times the men would lie at full length under the trees, in the soft summer twilight, smoking their pipes and drinking in the melodious utterances. An indistinct idea that this was pastoral happiness pervaded the camp. "This 'ere kind o' think," said the Cockney Simmons, meditatively reclining on his elbow, "is 'evingly." It reminded him of Greenwich.

On the long summer days The Luck was usually carried to the gulch, from whence the golden store of Roaring Camp was taken. There, on a blanket spread over pine-boughs, he would lie while the men were working in the ditches below. Latterly, there was a rude attempt to decorate this bower with flowers and sweet-smelling shrubs, and generally some one would bring him a cluster of wild honeysuckles, azaleas, or the painted blossoms of Las Mariposas. The men had suddenly awakened to the fact that there were beauty and significance in these trifles, which they had so long trodden carelessly beneath their feet. A flake of glittering mica, a fragment of variegated quartz, a bright pebble from the bed of the creek, became beautiful to eyes thus cleared and strengthened, and were invariably put aside for "The Luck." It was wonderful how many treasures the woods and hillsides yielded that " would do for Tommy." Surrounded by playthings such as never child out of fairy-land had before, it is to be hoped that Tommy was content. He appeared to be securely happy, albeit there was an infantine gravity about him, a contemplative light in his round gray eyes, that sometimes worried Stumpy. He was always tractable and quiet, and it is recorded that once, having crept beyond his "corral," — a hedge of tessellated pine-boughs, which surrounded his bed, — he dropped over the bank on his head in the soft earth, and remained with his mottled legs in the air in that position for at least five minutes with unflinching gravity. He was extricated without a murmur. I hesitate to record the many other instances of his sagacity, which rest, unfortunately, upon the statements of prejudiced friends. Some of them were not without a tinge of superstition. "I crep' up the bank just now," said Kentuck one day, in a breathless state of excitement, "and dern my skin if he was n't a talking to a jay-bird as was a sittin' on his lap. There they was, just as free and sociable as anything you please, a jawin' at each other just like two cherry-bums." Howbeit, whether creeping over the pine-boughs or lying lazily on his back blinking at the leaves above him, to him the birds sang, the squirrels chattered, and the flowers bloomed. Nature was his nurse and playfellow. For him she would let slip between the leaves golden shafts of sunlight that fell just within his grasp; she would send wandering breezes to visit him with the balm of bay and resinous gums; to him the tall red-woods nodded familiarly and sleepily, the bumble-bees buzzed, and the rooks cawed a slumbrous accompaniment.

Such was the golden summer of Roaring Camp. They were " flush times," — and the Luck was with them. The claims had yielded enormously. The camp was jealous of its privileges and looked suspiciously on strangers. No encouragement was given to immigration, and, to make their seclusion more perfect, the land on either side of the mountain wall that surrounded the camp they duly preempted. This, and a reputation for singular proficiency with the revolver, kept the reserve of Roaring Camp inviolate. The expressman — their only connecting link with the surrounding world — sometimes told wonderful stories of the camp. He would say, "They 've a street up there in 'Roaring,' that would lay over any street in Red Dog. They 've got vines and flowers round their houses, and they wash themselves twice a day. But they 're mighty rough on strangers, and they worship an Ingin baby."

With the prosperity of the camp came a desire for further improvement. It was proposed to build a hotel in the following spring, and to invite one or two decent families to reside there for the sake of "The Luck,"—who might perhaps profit by female companionship. The sacrifice that this concession to the sex cost these men, who were fiercely sceptical in regard to its general virtue and usefulness, can only be accounted for by their affection for Tommy. A few still held out. But the resolve could not be carried into effect for three months, and the minority meekly yielded in the hope that something might turn up to prevent it. And it did.

The winter of 1851 will long be remembered in the foot-hills. The snow lay deep on the Sierras, and every mountain creek became a river, and every river a lake. Each gorge and gulch was transformed into a tumultuous watercourse that descended the hillsides, tearing down giant trees and scattering its drift and débris along the plain. Red Dog had been twice under water, and Roaring Camp had been forewarned. "Water put the gold into them gulches," said Stumpy. "It's been here once and will be here again!" And that night the North Fork suddenly leaped over its banks, and swept up the triangular valley of Roaring Camp.

In the confusion of rushing water, crushing trees, and crackling timber, and the darkness which seemed to flow with the water and blot out the fair valley, but little could be done to collect the scattered camp. When the morning broke, the cabin of

Stumpy nearest the river-bank was gone. Higher up the gulch they found the body of its unlucky owner; but the pride, the hope, the joy, the Luck, of Roaring Camp had disappeared. They were returning with sad hearts, when a shout from the bank recalled them.

It was a relief-boat from down the river. They had picked up, they said, a man and an infant, nearly exhausted, about two miles below. Did anybody know them, and did they belong here?

It needed but a glance to show them Kentuck lying there, cruelly crushed and bruised, but still holding the Luck of Roaring Camp in his arms. As they bent over the strangely assorted pair, they saw that the child was cold and pulseless. "He is dead," said one. Kentuck opened his eyes. "Dead?" he repeated feebly. "Yes, my man, and you are dying too." A smile lit the eyes of the expiring Kentuck. "Dying," he repeated, "he's a taking me with him, — tell the boys I've got the Luck with me now"; and the strong man, clinging to the frail babe as a drowning man is said to cling to a straw, drifted away into the shadowy river that flows forever to the unknown sea.

THE OUTCASTS OF POKER FLAT.

AS Mr. John Oakhurst, gambler, stepped into the main street of Poker Flat on the morning of the twenty-third of November, 1850, he was conscious of a change in its moral atmosphere since the preceding night. Two or three men, conversing earnestly together, ceased as he approached, and exchanged significant glances. There was a Sabbath lull in the air, which, in a settlement unused to Sabbath influences, looked ominous.

Mr. Oakhurst's calm, handsome face betrayed small concern in these indications. Whether he was conscious of any predisposing cause, was another question. "I reckon they're after somebody," he reflected; "likely it's me." He returned to his pocket the handkerchief with which he had been whipping away the red dust of Poker Flat from his neat boots, and quietly discharged his mind of any further conjecture.

In point of fact, Poker Flat was "after somebody." It had lately suffered the loss of several thousand dollars, two valuable horses, and a prominent citizen. It was experiencing a spasm of virtuous reaction, quite as lawless and ungovernable as any of the acts that had provoked it. A secret committee had determined to rid the town of all improper persons. This was done permanently in regard of two men who were then hanging from the boughs of a sycamore in the gulch, and temporarily in the banishment of certain other objectionable characters. I regret to say that some of these were ladies. It is but due to the sex, however, to state that their impropriety was professional, and it was only in such easily established standards of evil that Poker Flat ventured to sit in judgment.

Mr. Oakhurst was right in supposing that he was included in this category. A few of the committee had urged hanging him as a possible example, and a sure method of reimbursing themselves from his pockets of the sums he had won from them. " It's agin justice," said Jim Wheeler, " to let this yer young man from Roaring Camp — an entire stranger — carry away our money." But a crude sentiment of equity residing in the breasts of those who had been fortunate enough to win from Mr. Oakhurst overruled this narrower local prejudice.

Mr. Oakhurst received his sentence with philosophic calmness, none the less coolly that he was aware of the hesitation of his judges. He was too much of a gambler not to accept Fate.

With him life was at best an uncertain game, and he recognized the usual percentage in favor of the dealer.

A body of armed men accompanied the deported wickedness of Poker Flat to the outskirts of the settlement. Besides Mr. Oakhurst, who was known to be a coolly desperate man, and for whose intimidation the armed escort was intended, the expatriated party consisted of a young woman familiarly known as "The Duchess"; another, who had won the title of "Mother Shipton"; and "Uncle Billy," a suspected sluice-robber and confirmed drunkard. The cavalcade provoked no comments from the spectators, nor was any word uttered by the escort. Only, when the gulch which marked the uttermost limit of Poker Flat was reached, the leader spoke briefly and to the point. The exiles were forbidden to return at the peril of their lives.

As the escort disappeared, their pent-up feelings found vent in a few hysterical tears from the Duchess, some bad language from Mother Shipton, and a Parthian volley of expletives from Uncle Billy. The philosophic Oakhurst alone remained silent. He listened calmly to Mother Shipton's desire to cut somebody's heart out, to the repeated statements of the Duchess that she would die in the road, and to the alarming oaths that seemed to be bumped out of Uncle

Billy as he rode forward. With the easy good-humor characteristic of his class, he insisted upon exchanging his own riding-horse, " Five Spot," for the sorry mule which the Duchess rode. But even this act did not draw the party into any closer sympathy. The young woman readjusted her somewhat draggled plumes with a feeble, faded coquetry; Mother Shipton eyed the possessor of " Five Spot" with malevolence, and Uncle Billy included the whole party in one sweeping anathema.

The road to Sandy Bar — a camp that, not having as yet experienced the regenerating influences of Poker Flat, consequently seemed to offer some invitation to the emigrants — lay over a steep mountain range. It was distant a day's severe travel. In that advanced season, the party soon passed out of the moist, temperate regions of the foot-hills into the dry, cold, bracing air of the Sierras. The trail was narrow and difficult. At noon the Duchess, rolling out of her saddle upon the ground, declared her intention of going no far-ther, and the party halted.

The spot was singularly wild and impressive. A wooded amphitheatre, surrounded on three sides by precipitous cliffs of naked granite, sloped gen-tly toward the crest of another precipice that over-looked the valley. It was, undoubtedly, the most suitable spot for a camp, had camping been advis-able. But Mr. Oakhurst knew that scarcely half

the journey to Sandy Bar was accomplished, and
the party were not equipped or provisioned for delay. This fact he pointed out to his companions
curtly, with a philosophic commentary on the folly
of "throwing up their hand before the game was
played out." But they were furnished with liquor,
which in this emergency stood them in place of
food, fuel, rest, and prescience. In spite of his
remonstrances, it was not long before they were
more or less under its influence. Uncle Billy
passed rapidly from a bellicose state into one of
stupor, the Duchess became maudlin, and Mother
Shipton snored. Mr. Oakhurst alone remained
erect, leaning against a rock, calmly surveying
them.

Mr. Oakhurst did not drink. It interfered with
a profession which required coolness, impassive-
ness, and presence of mind, and, in his own language, he "could n't afford it." As he gazed at
his recumbent fellow-exiles, the loneliness begot-
ten of his pariah-trade, his habits of life, his very
vices, for the first time seriously oppressed him.
He bestirred himself in dusting his black clothes,
washing his hands and face, and other acts characteristic of his studiously neat habits, and for a
moment forgot his annoyance. The thought of
deserting his weaker and more pitiable companions
never perhaps occurred to him. Yet he could not
help feeling the want of that excitement which,

singularly enough, was most conducive to that
calm equanimity for which he was notorious. He
looked at the gloomy walls that rose a thousand
feet sheer above the circling pines around him ;
at the sky, ominously clouded ; at the valley below, already deepening into shadow. And, doing
so, suddenly he heard his own name called.

A horseman slowly ascended the trail. In the
fresh, open face of the new-comer Mr. Oakhurst
recognized Tom Simson, otherwise known as " The
Innocent" of Sandy Bar. He had met him some
months before over a "little game," and had, with
perfect equanimity, won the entire fortune —
amounting to some forty dollars — of that guile-
less youth. After the game was finished, Mr.
Oakhurst drew the youthful speculator behind the
door and thus addressed him : " Tommy, you 're a
good little man, but you can't gamble worth a
cent. Don't try it over again." He then handed
'um his money back, pushed him gently from the
room, and so made a devoted slave of Tom Simson.

There was a remembrance of this in his boyish
and enthusiastic greeting of Mr. Oakhurst. He
had started, he said, to go to Poker Flat to seek his
fortune. " Alone ? " No, not exactly alone ; in
fact (a giggle), he had run away with Piney
Woods. Did n't Mr. Oakhurst remember Piney ?
She that used to wait on the table at the Tem-
perance House ? They had been engaged a long

time, but old Jake Woods had objected, and so they had run away, and were going to Poker Flat to be married, and here they were. And they were tired out, and how lucky it was they had found a place to camp and company. All this the Innocent delivered rapidly, while Piney, a stout, comely damsel of fifteen, emerged from behind the pine-tree, where she had been blushing unseen, and rode to the side of her lover.

Mr. Oakhurst seldom troubled himself with sentiment, still less with propriety; but he had a vague idea that the situation was not fortunate. He retained, however, his presence of mind sufficiently to kick Uncle Billy, who was about to say something, and Uncle Billy was sober enough to recognize in Mr. Oakhurst's kick a superior power that would not bear trifling. He then endeavored to dissuade Tom Simson from delaying further, but in vain. He even pointed out the fact that there was no provision, nor means of making a camp. But, unluckily, the Innocent met this objection by assuring the party that he was provided with an extra mule loaded with provisions, and by the discovery of a rude attempt at a log-house near the trail. "Piney can stay with Mrs. Oakhurst," said the Innocent, pointing to the Duchess, "and I can shift for myself."

Nothing but Mr. Oakhurst's admonishing foot saved Uncle Billy from bursting into a roar of

laughter. As it was, he felt compelled to retire
up the cañon until he could recover his gravity.
There he confided the joke to the tall pine-trees,
with many slaps of his leg, contortions of his face,
and the usual profanity. But when he returned
to the party, he found them seated by a fire — for
the air had grown strangely chill and the sky
overcast — in apparently amicable conversation.
Piney was actually talking in an impulsive, girlish
fashion to the Duchess, who was listening with an
interest and animation she had not shown for
many days. The Innocent was holding forth, apparently with equal effect, to Mr. Oakhurst and
Mother Shipton, who was actually relaxing into
amiability. "Is this yer a d—d picnic?" said
Uncle Billy, with inward scorn, as he surveyed the
sylvan group, the glancing firelight, and the tethered animals in the foreground. Suddenly an idea
mingled with the alcoholic fumes that disturbed
his brain. It was apparently of a jocular nature,
for he felt impelled to slap his leg again and cram
his fist into his mouth.

As the shadows crept slowly up the mountain,
a slight breeze rocked the tops of the pine-trees,
and moaned through their long and gloomy aisles.
The ruined cabin, patched and covered with pine-
boughs, was set apart for the ladies. As the lovers
parted, they unaffectedly exchanged a kiss, so honest and sincere that it might have been heard above

the swaying pines. The frail Duchess and the malevolent Mother Shipton were probably too stunned
to remark upon this last evidence of simplicity,
and so turned without a word to the hut. The
fire was replenished, the men lay down before the
door, and in a few minutes were asleep.

Mr. Oakhurst was a light sleeper. Toward morning he awoke benumbed and cold. As he stirred
the dying fire, the wind, which was now blowing
strongly, brought to his cheek that which caused
the blood to leave it, — snow !

He started to his feet with the intention of
awakening the sleepers, for there was no time to
lose. But turning to where Uncle Billy had been
lying, he found him gone. A suspicion leaped to
his brain and a curse to his lips. He ran to the
spot where the mules had been tethered ; they
were no longer there. The tracks were already
rapidly disappearing in the snow.

The momentary excitement brought Mr. Oakhurst back to the fire with his usual calm. He
did not waken the sleepers. The Innocent slum-
bered peacefully, with a smile on his good-humored,
freckled face ; the virgin Piney slept beside her
frailer sisters as sweetly as though attended by
celestial guardians, and Mr. Oakhurst, drawing his
blanket over his shoulders, stroked his mustaches
and waited for the dawn. It came slowly in a
whirling mist of snow-flakes, that dazzled and con-

fused the eye. What could be seen of the landscape appeared magically changed. He looked over
the valley, and summed up the present and future
in two words, — " snowed in ! "

A careful inventory of the provisions, which,
fortunately for the party, had been stored within
the hut, and so escaped the felonious fingers of
Uncle Billy, disclosed the fact that with care and
prudence they might last ten days longer. " That
is," said Mr. Oakhurst, *sotto voce* to the Innocent,
" if you 're willing to board us. If you ain't — and
perhaps you 'd better not — you can wait till Uncle
Billy gets back with provisions." For some occult
reason, Mr. Oakhurst could not bring himself to
disclose Uncle Billy's rascality, and so offered the
hypothesis that he had wandered from the camp
and had accidentally stampeded the animals. He
dropped a warning to the Duchess and Mother
Shipton, who of course knew the facts of their
associate's defection. " They 'll find out the truth
about us *all* when they find out anything," he
added, significantly, " and there 's no good frighten-
ing them now."

Tom Simson not only put all his worldly store
at the disposal of Mr. Oakhurst, but seemed to
enjoy the prospect of their enforced seclusion.
" We 'll have a good camp for a week, and then
the snow 'll melt, and we 'll all go back together."
The cheerful gayety of the young man, and Mr.

Oakhurst's calm infected the others. The Innocent, with the aid of pine-boughs, extemporized a thatch for the roofless cabin, and the Duchess directed Piney in the rearrangement of the interior with a taste and tact that opened the blue eyes of that provincial maiden to their fullest extent. " I r ckon now you 're used to fine things at Poker Flat," said Piney. The Duchess turned away sharply to conceal something that reddened her cheeks through its professional tint, and Mother Shipton requested Piney not to " chatter." But when Mr. Oakhurst returned from a weary search for the trail, he heard the sound of happy laughter echoed from the rocks. He stopped in some alarm, and his thoughts first naturally reverted to the whiskey, which he had prudently *caché*. " And yet it don't somehow sound like whiskey," said the gambler. It was not until he caught sight of the blazing fire through the still-blinding storm and the group around it that he settled to the conviction that it was " square fun."

Whether Mr. Oakhurst had *caché* his cards with the whiskey as something debarred the free access of the community, I cannot say. It was certain that, in Mother Shipton's words, he " did n't say cards once" during that evening. Haply the time was beguiled by an accordion, produced somewhat ostentatiously by Tom Simson from his pack. Notwithstanding some difficulties attending the manipulation of this instrument, Piney Woods managed to pluck several reluctant melodies from its keys, to an accompaniment by the Innocent on a pair of bone castinets. But the crowning festivity of the evening was reached in a rude camp-meeting hymn, which the lovers, joining hands, sang with great earnestness and vocifera- tion. I fear that a certain defiant tone and Cove- nanter's swing to its chorus, rather than any de- votional quality, caused it speedily to infect the others, who at last joined in the refrain: —

> " I 'm proud to live in the service of the Lord,
> And I 'm bound to die in His army."

The pines rocked, the storm eddied and whirled above the miserable group, and the flames of their altar leaped heavenward, as if in token of the vow.

At midnight the storm abated, the rolling clouds parted, and the stars glittered keenly above the sleeping camp. Mr. Oakhurst, whose professional habits had enabled him to live on the smallest possible amount of sleep, in dividing the watch with Tom Simson, somehow managed to take upon himself the greater part of that duty. He excused himself to the Innocent, by saying that he had " often been a week without sleep." " Doing what ? " asked Tom. " Poker ! " replied Oakhurst, sententiously; " when a man gets a streak of luck,

—nigger-luck,—he don't get tired. The luck gives in first. Luck," continued the gambler, reflectively, "is a mighty queer thing. All you know about it for certain is that it's bound to change. And it's finding out when it's going to change that makes you. We've had a streak of bad luck since we left Poker Flat,—you come along, and slap you get into it, too. If you can hold your cards right along you're all right. For," added the gambler, with cheerful irrelevance,—

"'I'm proud to live in the service of the Lord,
And I'm bound to die in His army.'"

The third day came, and the sun, looking through the white-curtained valley, saw the outcasts divide their slowly decreasing store of provisions for the morning meal. It was one of the peculiarities of that mountain climate that its rays diffused a kindly warmth over the wintry landscape, as if in regretful commiseration of the past. But it revealed drift on drift of snow piled high around the hut,—a hopeless, uncharted, trackless sea of white lying below the rocky shores to which the castaways still clung. Through the marvellously clear air the smoke of the pastoral village of Poker Flat rose miles away. Mother Shipton saw it, and from a remote pinnacle of her rocky fastness, hurled in that direction a final malediction. It was her last vituperative attempt, and perhaps for that reason was invested with a certain degree of sublimity. It did her good, she privately informed the Duchess. "Just you go out there and cuss, and see." She then set herself to the task of amusing "the child," as she and the Duchess were pleased to call Piney. Piney was no chicken, but it was a soothing and original theory of the pair thus to account for the fact that she did n't swear and was n't improper.

When night crept up again through the gorges, the reedy notes of the accordion rose and fell in fitful spasms and long-drawn gasps by the flickering camp-fire. But music failed to fill entirely the aching void left by insufficient food, and a new diversion was proposed by Piney, — story-telling. Neither Mr. Oakhurst nor his female companions caring to relate their personal experiences, this plan would have failed, too, but for the Innocent. Some months before he had chanced upon a stray copy of Mr. Pope's ingenious translation of the Iliad. He now proposed to narrate the principal incidents of that poem — having thoroughly mastered the argument and fairly forgotten the words — in the current vernacular of Sandy Bar. And so for the rest of that night the Homeric demigods again walked the earth. Trojan bully and wily Greek wrestled in the winds, and the great pines in the cañon seemed to bow to the wrath of the son of Peleus. Mr. Oakhurst listened with quiet satisfaction. Most especially was he interested in the fate of "Ash-heels," as the Innocent persisted in denominating the "swift-footed Achilles."

So with small food and much of Homer and the accordion, a week passed over the heads of the outcasts. The sun again forsook them, and again from leaden skies the snow-flakes were sifted over the land. Day by day closer around them drew the snowy circle, until at last they looked from their prison over drifted walls of dazzling white, that towered twenty feet above their heads. It became more and more difficult to replenish their fires, even from the fallen trees beside them, now half hidden in the drifts. And yet no one complained. The lovers turned from the dreary prospect and looked into each other's eyes, and were happy. Mr. Oakhurst settled himself coolly to the losing game before him. The Duchess, more cheerful than she had been, assumed the care of Piney. Only Mother Shipton — once the strongest of the party — seemed to sicken and fade. At midnight on the tenth day she called Oakhurst to her side. "I'm going," she said, in a voice of querulous weakness, "but don't say anything about it. Don't waken the kids. Take the bundle from under my head and open it." Mr. Oakhurst did so. It contained Mother Shipton's rations for the last week, untouched. "Give 'em to the child," she said, pointing to the sleeping Piney. "You've starved yourself," said the gambler. "That's what they call it," said the woman, querulously, as she lay down again, and, turning her face to the wall, passed quietly away.

The accordion and the bones were put aside that day, and Homer was forgotten. When the body of Mother Shipton had been committed to the snow, Mr. Oakhurst took the Innocent aside, and showed him a pair of snow-shoes, which he had fashioned from the old pack-saddle. "There's one chance in a hundred to save her yet," he said, pointing to Piney; "but it's there," he added, pointing toward Poker Flat. "If you can reach there in two days she's safe." "And you?" asked Tom Simson. "I'll stay here," was the curt reply.

The lovers parted with a long embrace. "You are not going, too?" said the Duchess, as she saw Mr. Oakhurst apparently waiting to accompany him. "As far as the cañon," he replied. He turned suddenly, and kissed the Duchess, leaving her pallid face aflame, and her trembling limbs rigid with amazement.

Night came, but not Mr. Oakhurst. It brought the storm again and the whirling snow. Then the Duchess, feeding the fire, found that some one had quietly piled beside the hut enough fuel to last a few days longer. The tears rose to her eyes, but she hid them from Piney.

The women slept but little. In the morning,

looking into each other's faces, they read their fate. Neither spoke; but Piney, accepting the position of the stronger, drew near and placed her arm around the Duchess's waist. They kept this attitude for the rest of the day. That night the storm reached its greatest fury, and, rending asunder the protecting pines, invaded the very hut.

Toward morning they found themselves unable to feed the fire, which gradually died away. As the embers slowly blackened, the Duchess crept closer to Piney, and broke the silence of many hours: " Piney, can you pray ? " " No, dear," said Piney, simply. The Duchess, without knowing exactly why, felt relieved, and, putting her head upon Piney's shoulder, spoke no more. And so reclining, the younger and purer pillowing the head of her soiled sister upon her virgin breast, they fell asleep.

The wind lulled as if it feared to waken them. Feathery drifts of snow, shaken from the long pine-boughs, flew like white-winged birds, and settled about them as they slept. The moon through the rifted clouds looked down upon what had been the camp. But all human stain, all trace of earthly travail, was hidden beneath the spotless mantle mercifully flung from above.

They slept all that day and the next, nor did they waken when voices and footsteps broke the silence of the camp. And when pitying fingers brushed the snow from their wan faces, you could scarcely have told from the equal peace that dwelt upon them, which was she that had sinned. Even the law of Poker Flat recognized this, and turned away, leaving them still locked in each other's arms.

But at the head of the gulch, on one of the largest pine-trees, they found the deuce of clubs pinned to the bark with a bowie-knife. It bore the following, written in pencil, in a firm hand:—

BENEATH THIS TREE
LIES THE BODY
OF
JOHN OAKHURST,
WHO STRUCK A STREAK OF BAD LUCK
ON THE 23D OF NOVEMBER, 1850,
AND
HANDED IN HIS CHECKS
ON THE 7TH DECEMBER, 1850.

And pulseless and cold, with a Derringer by his side and a bullet in his heart, though still calm as in life, beneath the snow lay he who was at once the strongest and yet the weakest of the outcasts of Poker Flat.

MIGGLES.

WE were eight, including the driver. We
had not spoken during the passage of the
last six miles, since the jolting of the heavy vehicle over the roughening road had spoiled the
Judge's last poetical quotation. The tall man beside the Judge was asleep, his arm passed through
the swaying strap and his head resting upon it, —
altogether a limp, helpless-looking object, as if he
had hanged himself and been cut down too late.
The French lady on the back seat was asleep, too,
yet in a half-conscious propriety of attitude, shown
even in the disposition of the handkerchief which
she held to her forehead and which partially veiled
her face. The lady from Virginia City, travelling
with her husband, had long since lost all individuality in a wild confusion of ribbons, veils,
furs, and shawls. There was no sound but the
rattling of wheels and the dash of rain upon the
roof. Suddenly the stage stopped and we became
dimly aware of voices. The driver was evidently
in the midst of an exciting colloquy with some
one in the road, — a colloquy of which such fragments as "bridge gone," "twenty feet of water,"

"can't pass," were occasionally distinguishable above the storm. Then came a lull, and a mysterious voice from the road shouted the parting adjuration, —

"Try Miggles's."

We caught a glimpse of our leaders as the vehicle slowly turned, of a horseman vanishing through the rain, and we were evidently on our way to Miggles's.

Who and where was Miggles? The Judge, our authority, did not remember the name, and he knew the country thoroughly. The Washoe traveller thought Miggles must keep a hotel. We only knew that we were stopped by high water in front and rear, and that Miggles was our rock of refuge. A ten minutes' splashing through a tangled by-road, scarcely wide enough for the stage, and we drew up before a barred and boarded gate in a wide stone wall or fence about eight feet high. Evidently Miggles's, and evidently Miggles did not keep a hotel.

The driver got down and tried the gate. It was securely locked.

"Miggles! O Miggles!"

No answer.

"Migg-ells! You Miggles!" continued the driver, with rising wrath.

"Migglesy!" joined in the expressman, persuasively. "O Miggy! Mig!"

But no reply came from the apparently insensate Miggles. The Judge, who had finally got the window down, put his head out and propounded a series of questions, which if answered categorically would have undoubtedly elucidated the whole mystery, but which the driver evaded by replying that "if we did n't want to sit in the coach all night, we had better rise up and sing out for Miggles."

So we rose up and called on Miggles in chorus; then separately. And when we had finished, a Hibernian fellow-passenger from the roof called for "Maygells!" whereat we all laughed. While we were laughing, the driver cried "Shoo!"

We listened. To our infinite amazement the chorus of "Miggles" was repeated from the other side of the wall, even to the final and supplemental "Maygells."

"Extraordinary echo," said the Judge.

"Extraordinary d—d skunk!" roared the driver, contemptuously. "Come out of that, Miggles, and show yourself! Be a man, Miggles! Don't hide in the dark; I would n't if I were you, Miggles," continued Yuba Bill, now dancing about in an excess of fury.

"Miggles!" continued the voice, "O Miggles!"

"My good man! Mr. Myghail!" said the Judge, softening the asperities of the name as much as possible. "Consider the inhospitality of refusing shelter from the inclemency of the weather to helpless females. Really, my dear sir —" But a succession of "Miggles," ending in a burst of laughter, drowned his voice.

Yuba Bill hesitated no longer. Taking a heavy stone from the road, he battered down the gate, and with the expressman entered the enclosure. We followed. Nobody was to be seen. In the gathering darkness all that we could distinguish was that we were in a garden — from the rose-bushes that scattered over us a minute spray from their dripping leaves — and before a long, ram-bling wooden building.

"Do you know this Miggles?" asked the Judge of Yuba Bill.

"No, nor don't want to," said Bill, shortly, who felt the Pioneer Stage Company insulted in his person by the contumacious Miggles.

"But, my dear sir," expostulated the Judge, as he thought of the barred gate.

"Lookee here," said Yuba Bill, with fine irony, "had n't you better go back and sit in the coach till yer introduced? I'm going in," and he pushed open the door of the building.

A long room lighted only by the embers of a fire that was dying on the large hearth at its fur-ther extremity; the walls curiously papered, and the flickering firelight bringing out its grotesque pattern; somebody sitting in a large arm-chair by the fireplace. All this we saw as we crowded together into the room, after the driver and expressman.

"Hello, be you Miggles?" said Yuba Bill to the solitary occupant.

The figure neither spoke nor stirred. Yuba Bill walked wrathfully toward it, and turned the eye of his coach-lantern upon its face. It was a man's face, prematurely old and wrinkled, with very large eyes, in which there was that expression of perfectly gratuitous solemnity which I had sometimes seen in an owl's. The large eyes wandered from Bill's face to the lantern, and finally fixed their gaze on that luminous object, without further recognition.

Bill restrained himself with an effort.

"Miggles! Be you deaf? You ain't dumb anyhow, you know"; and Yuba Bill shook the insensate figure by the shoulder.

To our great dismay, as Bill removed his hand, the venerable stranger apparently collapsed, — sinking into half his size and an undistinguishable heap of clothing.

"Well, dern my skin," said Bill, looking appealingly at us, and hopelessly retiring from the contest.

The Judge now stepped forward, and we lifted the mysterious invertebrate back into his original position. Bill was dismissed with the lantern to reconnoitre outside, for it was evident that from the helplessness of this solitary man there must be attendants near at hand, and we all drew around the fire. The Judge, who had regained his authority, and had never lost his conversational amiability, — standing before us with his back to the hearth, — charged us, as an imaginary jury, as follows : —

"It is evident that either our distinguished friend here has reached that condition described by Shakespeare as 'the sere and yellow leaf,' or has suffered some premature abatement of his mental and physical faculties. Whether he is really the Miggles — "

Here he was interrupted by " Miggles ! O Miggles ! Migglesy ! Mig !" and, in fact, the whole chorus of Miggles in very much the same key as it had once before been delivered unto us.

We gazed at each other for a moment in some alarm. The Judge, in particular, vacated his position quickly, as the voice seemed to come directly over his shoulder. The cause, however, was soon discovered in a large magpie who was perched upon a shelf over the fireplace, and who immediately relapsed into a sepulchral silence, which contrasted singularly with his previous volubility. It was, undoubtedly, his voice which we had heard in the road, and our friend in the chair was not responsible for the discourtesy.

Yuba Bill, who re-entered the room after an unsuccessful search, was loath to accept the explanation, and still eyed the helpless sitter with suspicion. He had found a shed in which he had put up his horses, but he came back dripping and sceptical. "Thar ain't nobody but him within ten mile of the shanty, and that 'ar d—d old skeesicks knows it."

But the faith of the majority proved to be securely based. Bill had scarcely ceased growling before we heard a quick step upon the porch, the trailing of a wet skirt, the door was flung open, and with a flash of white teeth, a sparkle of dark eyes, and an utter absence of ceremony or diffidence, a young woman entered, shut the door, and, panting, leaned back against it.

"O, if you please, I'm Miggles!"

And this was Miggles! this bright-eyed, full-throated young woman, whose wet gown of coarse blue stuff could not hide the beauty of the feminine curves to which it clung; from the chestnut crown of whose head, topped by a man's oil-skin sou'wester, to the little feet and ankles, hidden somewhere in the recesses of her boy's brogans, all was grace;— this was Miggles, laughing at us, too, in the most airy, frank, off-hand manner imaginable.

"You see, boys," said she, quite out of breath, and holding one little hand against her side, quite

unheeding the speechless discomfiture of our party, or the complete demoralization of Yuba Bill,
whose features had relaxed into an expression of
gratuitous and imbecile cheerfulness, — " you see,
boys, I was mor'n two miles away when you
passed down the road. I thought you might pull
up here, and so I ran the whole way, knowing
nobody was home but Jim, — and — and — I 'm
out of breath — and — that lets me out."

And here Miggles caught her dripping oil-skin
hat from her head, with a mischievous swirl that
scattered a shower of rain-drops over us; attempted to put back her hair; dropped two hair-
pins in the attempt; laughed and sat down beside
Yuba Bill, with her hands crossed lightly on her
lap.

The Judge recovered himself first, and essayed
an extravagant compliment.

" I 'll trouble you for that thar har-pin," said
Miggles, gravely. Half a dozen hands were eagerly
stretched forward; the missing hair-pin was restored to its fair owner; and Miggles, crossing the
room, looked keenly in the face of the invalid.
The solemn eyes looked back at hers with an expression we had never seen before. Life and intelligence seemed to struggle back into the rugged
face. Miggles laughed again, — it was a singularly
eloquent laugh, — and turned her black eyes and
white teeth once more toward us.

" This afflicted person is — " hesitated the Judge.

" Jim," said Miggles.

" Your father ? "

" No."

" Brother ? "

" No."

" Husband ? "

Miggles darted a quick, half-defiant glance at the two lady passengers who I had noticed did not participate in the general masculine admiration of Miggles, and said, gravely, " No; it's Jim."

There was an awkward pause. The lady passengers moved closer to each other; the Washoe husband looked abstractedly at the fire; and the tall man apparently turned his eyes inward for self-support at this emergency. But Miggles's laugh, which was very infectious, broke the silence. " Come," she said briskly, " you must be hungry. Who 'll bear a hand to help me get tea ? "

She had no lack of volunteers. In a few moments Yuba Bill was engaged like Caliban in bearing logs for this Miranda; the expressman was grinding coffee on the veranda; to myself the arduous duty of slicing bacon was assigned; and the Judge lent each man his good-humored and voluble counsel. And when Miggles, assisted by the Judge and our Hibernian " deck passen-

ger," set the table with all the available crock-
ery, we had become quite joyous, in spite of the
rain that beat against windows, the wind that
whirled down the chimney, the two ladies who
whispered together in the corner, or the magpie
who uttered a satirical and croaking commentary
on their conversation from his perch above. In
the now bright, blazing fire we could see that
the walls were papered with illustrated journals,
arranged with feminine taste and discrimination.
The furniture was extemporized, and adapted from
candle-boxes and packing-cases, and covered with
gay calico, or the skin of some animal. The
arm-chair of the helpless Jim was an ingenious
variation of a flour-barrel. There was neatness,
and even a taste for the picturesque, to be seen in
the few details of the long low room.

The meal was a culinary success. But more, it
was a social triumph, — chiefly, I think, owing to
the rare tact of Miggles in guiding the conversation, asking all the questions herself, yet bearing
throughout a frankness that rejected the idea of
any concealment on her own part, so that we talked
of ourselves, of our prospects, of the journey, of
the weather, of each other, — of everything but
our host and hostess. It must be confessed that
Miggles's conversation was never elegant, rarely
grammatical, and that at times she employed expletives, the use of which had generally been yielded

to our sex. But they were delivered with such a lighting up of teeth and eyes, and were usually followed by a laugh — a laugh peculiar to Miggles — so frank and honest that it seemed to clear the moral atmosphere.

Once, during the meal, we heard a noise like the rubbing of a heavy body against the outer walls of the house. This was shortly followed by a scratching and sniffling at the door. "That's Joaquin," said Miggles, in reply to our questioning glances; "would you like to see him?" Before we could answer she had opened the door, and disclosed a half-grown grizzly, who instantly raised himself on his haunches, with his forepaws hanging down in the popular attitude of mendicancy, and looked admiringly at Miggles, with a very singular resemblance in his manner to Yuba Bill. "That's my watch-dog," said Miggles, in explanation. "O, he don't bite," she added, as the two lady passengers fluttered into a corner. "Does he, old Toppy?" (the latter remark being addressed directly to the sagacious Joaquin.) "I tell you what, boys," continued Miggles, after she had fed and closed the door on *Ursa Minor*, "you were in big luck that Joaquin was n't hanging round when you dropped in to-night." "Where was he?" asked the Judge. "With me," said Miggles. "Lord love you; he trots round with me nights like as if he was a man."

We were silent for a few moments, and listened to the wind. Perhaps we all had the same picture before us, — of Miggles walking through the rainy woods, with her savage guardian at her side. The Judge, I remember, said something about Una and her lion; but Miggles received it as she did other compliments, with quiet gravity. Whether she was altogether unconscious of the admiration she excited, — she could hardly have been oblivious of Yuba Bill's adoration, — I know not; but her very frankness suggested a perfect sexual equality that was cruelly humiliating to the younger members of our party.

The incident of the bear did not add anything in Miggles's favor to the opinions of those of her own sex who were present. In fact, the repast over, a chillness radiated from the two lady passengers that no pine-boughs brought in by Yuba Bill and cast as a sacrifice upon the hearth could wholly overcome. Miggles felt it; and, suddenly declaring that it was time to " turn in," offered to show the ladies to their bed in an adjoining room. " You, boys, will have to camp out here by the fire as well as you can," she added, " for thar ain't but the one room."

Our sex — by which, my dear sir, I allude of course to the stronger portion of humanity — has been generally relieved from the imputation of curiosity, or a fondness for gossip. Yet I am con-

strained to say, that hardly had the door closed on
Miggles than we crowded together, whispering,
snickering, smiling, and exchanging suspicions,·
surmises, and a thousand speculations in regard to
our pretty hostess and her singular companion. I
fear that we even hustled that imbecile paralytic,
who sat like a voiceless Memnon in our midst,
gazing with the serene indifference of the Past in
his passionless eyes upon our wordy counsels. In
the midst of an exciting discussion the door opened
again, and Miggles re-entered.

But not, apparently, the same Miggles who a
few hours before had flashed upon us. Her eyes
were downcast, and as she hesitated for a moment
on the threshold, with a blanket on her arm, she
seemed to have left behind her the frank fearless-
ness which had charmed us a moment before.
Coming into the room, she drew a low stool beside
the paralytic's chair, sat down, drew the blanket
over her shoulders, and saying, " If it 's all the same
to you, boys, as we 're rather crowded, I 'll stop
here to-night," took the invalid's withered hand in
her own, and turned her eyes upon the dying fire.
An instinctive feeling that this was only premoni-
tory to more confidential relations, and perhaps
some shame at our previous curiosity, kept us silent. The rain still beat upon the roof, wandering gusts of wind stirred the embers into momentary brightness, until, in a lull of the elements,

Miggles suddenly lifted up her head, and, throwing her hair over her shoulder, turned her face upon the group and asked, —

"Is there any of you that knows me?"

There was no reply.

"Think again! I lived at Marysville in '53. Everybody knew me there, and everybody had the right to know me. I kept the Polka Saloon until I came to live with Jim. That's six years ago. Perhaps I've changed some."

The absence of recognition may have disconcerted her. She turned her head to the fire again, and it was some seconds before she again spoke, and then more rapidly : —

"Well, you see I thought some of you must have known me. There's no great harm done, anyway. What I was going to say was this : Jim here" — she took his hand in both of hers as she spoke — "used to know me, if you did n't, and spent a heap of money upon me. I reckon he spent all he had. And one day — it's six years ago this winter — Jim came into my back room, sat down on my sofy, like as you see him in that chair, and never moved again without help. He was struck all of a heap, and never seemed to know what ailed him. The doctors came and said as how it was caused all along of his way of life, — for Jim was mighty free and wild like, — and that he would never get better, and could n't last

long anyway. They advised me to send him to
Frisco to the hospital, for he was no good to any
one and would be a baby all his life. Perhaps it
was something in Jim's eye, perhaps it was that I
never had a baby, but I said 'No.' I was rich
then, for I was popular with everybody, — gentlemen like yourself, sir, came to see me, — and I
sold out my business and bought this yer place,
because it was sort of out of the way of travel, you
see, and I brought my baby here."

With a woman's intuitive tact and poetry, she
had, as she spoke, slowly shifted her position so as
to bring the mute figure of the ruined man between her and her audience, hiding in the shadow
behind it, as if she offered it as a tacit apology
for her actions. Silent and expressionless, it yet
spoke for her ; helpless, crushed, and smitten with
the Divine thunderbolt, it still stretched an in-
visible arm around her.

Hidden in the darkness, but still holding his
hand, she went on : —

" It was a long time before I could get the hang
of things about yer, for I was used to company
and excitement. I could n't get any woman to
help me, and a man I dursent trust ; but what
with the Indians hereabout, who 'd do odd jobs for
me, and having everything sent from the North
Fork, Jim and I managed to worry through. The
Doctor would run up from Sacramento once in a

while. He'd ask to see 'Miggles's baby,' as he called Jim, and when he'd go away, he'd say, 'Miggles; you're a trump, — God bless you'; and it did n't seem so lonely after that. But the last time he was here he said, as he opened the door to go, 'Do you know, Miggles, your baby will grow up to be a man yet and an honor to his mother; but not here, Miggles, not here!' And I thought he went away sad, — and — and — " and here Miggles's voice and head were somehow both lost completely in the shadow.

"The folks about here are very kind," said Miggles, after a pause, coming a little into the light again. "The men from the fork used to hang around here, until they found they was n't wanted, and the women are kind, — and don't call. I was pretty lonely until I picked up Joaquin in the woods yonder one day, when he was n't so high, and taught him to beg for his dinner; and then thar's Polly — that's the magpie — she knows no end of tricks, and makes it quite sociable of evenings with her talk, and so I don't feel like as I was the only living being about the ranch. And Jim here," said Miggles, with her old laugh again, and coming out quite into the firelight, "Jim — why, boys, you would admire to see how much he knows for a man like him. Sometimes I bring him flowers, and he looks at 'em just as natural as if he knew 'em; and times, when we're sitting alone, I read him those things on the wall. Why, Lord!" said Miggles, with her frank laugh, "I've read him that whole side of the house this winter. There never was such a man for reading as Jim."

"Why," asked the Judge, "do you not marry this man to whom you have devoted your youthful life?"

"Well, you see," said Miggles, "it would be playing it rather low down on Jim, to take advantage of his being so helpless. And then, too, if we were man and wife, now, we'd both know that I was *bound* to do what I do now of my own accord."

"But you are young yet and attractive —"

"It's getting late," said Miggles, gravely, "and you'd better all turn in. Good-night, boys"; and, throwing the blanket over her head, Miggles laid herself down beside Jim's chair, her head pillowed on the low stool that held his feet, and spoke no more. The fire slowly faded from the hearth; we each sought our blankets in silence; and presently there was no sound in the long room but the pattering of the rain upon the roof, and the heavy breathing of the sleepers.

It was nearly morning when I awoke from a troubled dream. The storm had passed, the stars were shining, and through the shutterless window the full moon, lifting itself over the solemn pines without, looked into the room. It touched the lonely figure in the chair with an infinite compassion, and seemed to baptize with a shining flood the lowly head of the woman whose hair, as in the sweet old story, bathed the feet of him she loved. It even lent a kindly poetry to the rugged outline of Yuba Bill, half reclining on his elbow between them and his passengers, with savagely patient eyes keeping watch and ward. And then I fell asleep and only woke at broad day, with Yuba Bill standing over me, and "All aboard" ringing in my ears.

Coffee was waiting for us on the table, but Miggles was gone. We wandered about the house and lingered long after the horses were harnessed, but she did not return. It was evident that she wished to avoid a formal leave-taking, and had so left us to depart as we had come. After we had helped the ladies into the coach, we returned to the house and solemnly shook hands with the paralytic Jim, as solemnly settling him back into position after each hand-shake. Then we looked for the last time around the long low room, at the stool where Miggles had sat, and slowly took our seats in the waiting coach. The whip cracked, and we were off!

But as we reached the high-road, Bill's dexterous hand laid the six horses back on their haunches, and the stage stopped with a jerk. For there, on a little eminence beside the road, stood Miggles, her hair flying, her eyes sparkling, her white hand-kerchief waving, and her white teeth flashing a last "good-by." We waved our hats in return. And then Yuba Bill, as if fearful of further fasci-nation, madly lashed his horses forward, and we sank back in our seats. We exchanged not a word until we reached the North Fork, and the stage drew up at the Independence House. Then, the Judge leading, we walked into the bar-room and took our places gravely at the bar.

"Are your glasses charged, gentlemen?" said the Judge, solemnly taking off his white hat.

They were.

"Well, then, here's to *Miggles*. GOD BLESS HER!"

Perhaps He had. Who knows?

TENNESSEE'S PARTNER.

I DO not think that we ever knew his real name. Our ignorance of it certainly never gave us any social inconvenience, for at Sandy Bar in 1854 most men were christened anew. Sometimes these appellatives were derived from some distinctiveness of dress, as in the case of " Dungaree Jack "; or from some peculiarity of habit, as shown in " Saleratus Bill," so called from an undue proportion of that chemical in his daily bread ; or from some unlucky slip, as exhibited in "The Iron Pirate," a mild, inoffensive man, who earned that baleful title by his unfortunate mispronunciation of the term " iron pyrites." Perhaps this may have been the beginning of a rude heraldry ; but I am constrained to think that it was because a man's real name in that day rested solely upon his own unsupported statement. " Call yourself Clifford, do you ? " said Boston, addressing a timid new-comer with infinite scorn ; " hell is full of such Cliffords ! " He then introduced the unfortunate man, whose name happened to be really Clifford, as " Jay-bird Charley," — an unhallowed inspiration of the moment, that clung to him ever after.

But to return to Tennessee's Partner, whom we never knew by any other than this relative title; that he had ever existed as a separate and distinct individuality we only learned later. It seems that in 1853 he left Poker Flat to go to San Francisco, ostensibly to procure a wife. He never got any farther than Stockton. At that place he was attracted by a young person who waited upon the table at the hotel where he took his meals. One morning he said something to her which caused her to smile not unkindly, to somewhat coquettishly break a plate of toast over his upturned, serious, simple face, and to retreat to the kitchen. He followed her, and emerged a few moments later, covered with more toast and victory. That day week they were married by a Justice of the Peace, and returned to Poker Flat. I am aware that something more might be made of this episode, but I prefer to tell it as it was current at Sandy Bar, — in the gulches and bar-rooms, — where all sentiment was modified by a strong sense of humor.

Of their married felicity but little is known, perhaps for the reason that Tennessee, then living with his partner, one day took occasion to say something to the bride on his own account, at which, it is said, she smiled not unkindly and chastely retreated, — this time as far as Marysville, where Tennessee followed her, and where they went to housekeeping without the aid of a Justice

of the Peace. Tennessee's Partner took the loss of
his wife simply and seriously, as was his fashion.
But to everybody's surprise, when Tennessee one
day returned from Marysville, without his partner's
wife, — she having smiled and retreated with somebody else, — Tennessee's Partner was the first man
to shake his hand and greet him with affection.
The boys who had gathered in the cañon to see
the shooting were naturally indignant. Their in-
dignation might have found vent in sarcasm but
for a certain look in Tennessee's Partner's eye that
indicated a lack of humorous appreciation. In
fact, he was a grave man, with a steady applica-
tion to practical detail which was unpleasant in a
difficulty.

Meanwhile a popular feeling against Tennessee
had grown up on the Bar. He was known to be a
gambler; he was suspected to be a thief. In
these suspicions Tennessee's Partner was equally
compromised; his continued intimacy with Tennessee after the affair above quoted could only be
accounted for on the hypothesis of a copartnership
of crime. At last Tennessee's guilt became fla-
grant. One day he overtook a stranger on his way
to Red Dog. The stranger afterward related that
Tennessee beguiled the time with interesting anec-
dote and reminiscence, but illogically concluded
the interview in the following words : " And now,
young man, I 'll trouble you for your knife, your

pistols, and your money. You see your weppings might get you into trouble at Red Dog, and your money's a temptation to the evilly disposed. I think you said your address was San Francisco. I shall endeavor to call." It may be stated here that Tennessee had a fine flow of humor, which no business preoccupation could wholly subdue.

This exploit was his last. Red Dog and Sandy Bar made common cause against the highwayman. Tennessee was hunted in very much the same fashion as his prototype, the grizzly. As the toils closed around him, he made a desperate dash through the Bar, emptying his revolver at the crowd before the Arcade Saloon, and so on up Grizzly Cañon; but at its farther extremity he was stopped by a small man on a gray horse. The men looked at each other a moment in silence. Both were fearless, both self-possessed and independent; and both types of a civilization that in the seventeenth century would have been called heroic, but, in the nineteenth, simply "reckless." "What have you got there? — I call," said Tennessee, quietly. "Two bowers and an ace," said the stranger, as quietly, showing two revolvers and a bowie-knife. "That takes me," returned Tennessee; and with this gamblers' epigram, he threw away his useless pistol, and rode back with his captor.

It was a warm night. The cool breeze which

usually sprang up with the going down of the sun behind the *chaparral*-crested mountain was that evening withheld from Sandy Bar. The little cañon was stifling with heated resinous odors, and the decaying drift-wood on the Bar sent forth faint, sickening exhalations. The feverishness of day, and its fierce passions, still filled the camp. Lights moved restlessly along the bank of the river, striking no answering reflection from its tawny current. Against the blackness of the pines the windows of the old loft above the express-office stood out staringly bright; and through their curtainless panes the loungers below could see the forms of those who were even then deciding the fate of Tennessee. And above all this, etched on the dark firmament, rose the Sierra, remote and passionless, crowned with remoter passionless stars.

The trial of Tennessee was conducted as fairly as was consistent with a judge and jury who felt themselves to some extent obliged to justify, in their verdict, the previous irregularities of arrest and indictment. The law of Sandy Bar was implacable, but not vengeful. The excitement and personal feeling of the chase were over; with Tennessee safe in their hands they were ready to listen patiently to any defence, which they were already satisfied was insufficient. There being no doubt in their own minds, they were willing to give the prisoner the benefit of any that might exist. Se-

cure in the hypothesis that he ought to be hanged,
on general principles, they indulged him with more
latitude of defence than his reckless hardihood
seemed to ask.   The Judge appeared to be more
anxious than the prisoner, who, otherwise uncon-
cerned, evidently took a grim pleasure in the responsibility he had created.   "I don't take any
hand in this yer game," had been his invariable,
but good-humored reply to all questions.   The
Judge — who was also his captor — for a moment
vaguely regretted that he had not shot him "on
sight," that morning, but presently dismissed this
human weakness as unworthy of the judicial mind.
Nevertheless, when there was a tap at the door,
and it was said that Tennessee's Partner was
there on behalf of the prisoner, he was admitted at
once without question.   Perhaps the younger members of the jury, to whom the proceedings were
becoming irksomely thoughtful, hailed him as a
relief.

For he was not, certainly, an imposing figure.
Short and stout, with a square face, sunburned
into a preternatural redness, clad in a loose duck
"jumper," and trousers streaked and splashed
with red soil, his aspect under any circumstances
would have been quaint, and was now even ridiculous.   As he stooped to deposit at his feet a heavy
carpet-bag he was carrying, it became obvious,
from partially developed legends and inscriptions,

that the material with which his trousers had been
patched had been originally intended for a less
ambitious covering. Yet he advanced with great
gravity, and after having shaken the hand of each
person in the room with labored cordiality, he
wiped his serious, perplexed face on a red bandanna
handkerchief, a shade lighter than his complexion,
laid his powerful hand upon the table to steady
himself, and thus addressed the Judge : —

"I was passin' by," he began, by way of apology,
"and I thought I'd just step in and see how things
was gittin' on with Tennessee thar, — my pardner.
It's a hot night. I disremember any sich weather
before on the Bar."

He paused a moment, but nobody volunteering
any other meteorological recollection, he again had
recourse to his pocket-handkerchief, and for some
moments mopped his face diligently.

"Have you anything to say in behalf of the
prisoner?" said the Judge, finally.

"Thet's it," said Tennessee's Partner, in a tone
of relief. "I come yar as Tennessee's pardner, —
knowing him nigh on four year, off and on, wet
and dry, in luck and out o' luck. His ways ain't
allers my ways, but thar ain't any p'ints in that
young man, thar ain't any liveliness as he's been up
to, as I don't know. And you sez to me, sez you, —
confidential-like, and between man and man, — sez
you, 'Do you know anything in his behalf?' and I

sez to you, sez I, — confidential-like, as between
man and man, — 'What should a man know of his
pardner ? ' "

"Is this all you have to say ?" asked the Judge,
impatiently, feeling, perhaps, that a dangerous
sympathy of humor was beginning to humanize
the Court.

"Thet's so," continued Tennessee's Partner.
" It ain't for me to say anything agin' him. And
now, what's the case ? Here's Tennessee wants
money, wants it bad, and does n't like to ask it of
his old pardner. Well, what does Tennessee do ?
He lays for a stranger, and he fetches that stranger.
And you lays for *him*, and you fetches *him ;* and
the honors is easy. And I put it to you, bein' a
far-minded man, and to you, gentlemen, all, as
far-minded men, ef this is n't so."

"Prisoner," said the Judge, interrupting, " have
you any questions to ask this man ? "

" No ! no ! " continued Tennessee's Partner,
hastily. "I play this yer hand alone. To come
down to the bed-rock, it's just this : Tennessee,
thar, has played it pretty rough and expensive-
like on a stranger, and on this yer camp. And
now, what's the fair thing ? Some would say
more ; some would say less. Here's seventeen
hundred dollars in coarse gold and a watch, — it's
about all my pile, — and call it square ! " And
before a hand could be raised to prevent him, he

had emptied the contents of the carpet-bag upon the table.

For a moment his life was in jeopardy. One or two men sprang to their feet, several hands groped for hidden weapons, and a suggestion to "throw him from the window" was only overridden by a gesture from the Judge. Tennessee laughed. And apparently oblivious of the excitement, Tennessee's Partner improved the opportunity to mop his face again with his handkerchief.

When order was restored, and the man was made to understand, by the use of forcible figures and rhetoric, that Tennessee's offence could not be condoned by money, his face took a more serious and sanguinary hue, and those who were nearest to him noticed that his rough hand trembled slightly on the table. He hesitated a moment as he slowly returned the gold to the carpet-bag, as if he had not yet entirely caught the elevated sense of justice which swayed the tribunal, and was perplexed with the belief that he had not offered enough. Then he turned to the Judge, and saying, " This yer is a lone hand, played alone, and without my pardner," he bowed to the jury and was about to withdraw, when the Judge called him back. " If you have anything to say to Tennessee, you had better say it now." For the first time that evening the eyes of the prisoner and his strange advocate met. Tennessee smiled, showed his white teeth, and, saying, " Euchred, old man !" held out his hand.   Tennessee's Partner took it in his own, and saying, " I just dropped in as I was passin' to see how things was gettin' on," let the hand passively fall, and adding that " it was a warm night," again mopped his face with his handkerchief, and without another word withdrew.

The two men never again met each other alive. For the unparalleled insult of a bribe offered to Judge Lynch — who, whether bigoted, weak, or narrow, was at least incorruptible — firmly fixed in the mind of that mythical personage any wavering determination of Tennessee's fate ; and at the break of day he was marched, closely guarded, to meet it at the top of Marley's Hill.

How he met it, how cool he was, how he refused to say anything, how perfect were the arrangements of the committee, were all duly reported, with the addition of a warning moral and example to all future evil-doers, in the Red Dog Clarion, by its editor, who was present, and to whose vigorous English I cheerfully refer the reader. But the•beauty of that midsummer morning, the blessed amity of earth and air and sky, the awakened life of the free woods and hills, the joyous renewal and promise of Nature, and above all, the infinite Serenity that thrilled through each, was not reported, as not being a part of the social lesson.   And yet, when the weak and foolish deed

E

was done, and a life, with its possibilities and re-
sponsibilities, had passed out of the misshapen
thing that dangled between earth and sky, the
birds sang, the flowers bloomed, the sun shone,
as cheerily as before ; and possibly the Red Dog
Clarion was right.

Tennessee's Partner was not in the group that
surrounded the ominous tree. But as they turned
to disperse attention was drawn to the singular
appearance of a motionless donkey-cart halted at
the side of the road. As they approached, they at
once recognized the venerable " Jenny " and the
two-wheeled cart as the property of Tennessee's
Partner, — used by him in carrying dirt from his
claim ; and a few paces distant the owner of the
equipage himself, sitting under a buckeye-tree,
wiping the perspiration from his glowing face. In
answer to an inquiry, he said he had come for
the body of the " diseased," " if it was all the
same to the committee." He did n't wish to
" hurry anything " ; he could " wait." He was not
working that day ; and when the gentlemen were
done with the " diseased," he would take him.
" Ef thar is any present," he added, in his simple,
serious way, " as would care to jine in the fun'l,
they kin come." Perhaps it was from a sense of
humor, which I have already intimated was a
feature of Sandy Bar, — perhaps it was from something even better than that ; but two thirds of
the loungers accepted the invitation at once.

It was noon when the body of Tennessee was delivered into the hands of his partner. As the cart drew up to the fatal tree, we noticed that it contained a rough, oblong box, — apparently made from a section of sluicing, — and half filled with bark and the tassels of pine. The cart was further decorated with slips of willow, and made fragrant with buckeye-blossoms. When the body was deposited in the box, Tennessee's Partner drew over it a piece of tarred canvas, and gravely mounting the narrow seat in front, with his feet upon the shafts, urged the little donkey forward. The equipage moved slowly on, at that decorous pace which was habitual with "Jenny" even under less solemn circumstances. The men — half curiously, half jestingly, but all good-humoredly — strolled along beside the cart ; some in advance, some a little in the rear of the homely catafalque. But, whether from the narrowing of the road or some present sense of decorum, as the cart passed on, the company fell to the rear in couples, keeping step, and otherwise assuming the external show of a formal procession. Jack Folinsbee, who had at the outset played a funeral march in dumb show upon an imaginary trombone, desisted, from a lack of sympathy and appreciation, — not having, perhaps, your true humorist's capacity to be content with the enjoyment of his own fun.

The way led through Grizzly Cañon, — by this

time clothed in funereal drapery and shadows.
The redwoods, burying their moccasoned feet in
the red soil, stood in Indian-file along the track,
trailing an uncouth benediction from their bending
boughs upon the passing bier. A hare, surprised
into helpless inactivity, sat upright and pulsating
in the ferns by the roadside, as the *cortége* went
by. Squirrels hastened to gain a secure outlook
from higher boughs; and the blue-jays, spreading
their wings, fluttered before them like outriders,
until the outskirts of Sandy Bar were reached,
and the solitary cabin of Tennessee's Partner.

Viewed under more favorable circumstances, it
would not have been a cheerful place. The un-
picturesque site, the rude and unlovely outlines,
the unsavory details, which distinguish the nest-
building of the California miner, were all here,
with the dreariness of decay superadded. A few
paces from the cabin there was a rough enclosure,
which, in the brief days of Tennessee's Partner's
matrimonial felicity, had been used as a garden,
but was now overgrown with fern. As we approached it we were surprised to find that what
we had taken for a recent attempt at cultivation
was the broken soil about an open grave.

The cart was halted before the enclosure ; and
rejecting the offers of assistance with the same air
of simple self-reliance he had displayed throughout, Tennessee's Partner lifted the rough coffin on

his back, and deposited it, unaided, within the shallow grave. He then nailed down the board which served as a lid; and mounting the little mound of earth beside it, took off his hat, and slowly mopped his face with his handkerchief. This the crowd felt was a preliminary to speech; and they disposed themselves variously on stumps and boulders, and sat expectant.

"When a man," began Tennessee's Partner, slowly, "has been running free all day, what's the natural thing for him to do? Why, to come home. And if he ain't in a condition to go home, what can his best friend do? Why, bring him home! And here's Tennessee has been running free, and we brings him home from his wandering." He paused, and picked up a fragment of quartz, rubbed it thoughtfully on his sleeve, and went on: "It ain't the first time that I've packed him on my back, as you see'd me now. It ain't the first time that I brought him to this yer cabin when he could n't help himself; it ain't the first time that I and 'Jinny' have waited for him on yon hill, and picked him up and so fetched him home, when he could n't speak, and did n't know me. And now that it's the last time, why —" he paused, and rubbed the quartz gently on his sleeve — "you see it's sort of rough on his pardner. And now, gentlemen," he added, abruptly, picking up his long-handled shovel, "the fun'l's over;

and my thanks, and Tennessee's thanks, to you for your trouble."

Resisting any proffers of assistance, he began to fill in the grave, turning his back upon the crowd, that after a few moments' hesitation gradually withdrew. As they crossed the little ridge that hid Sandy Bar from view, some, looking back, thought they could see Tennessee's Partner, his work done, sitting upon the grave, his shovel between his knees, and his face buried in his red bandanna handkerchief. But it was argued by others that you could n't tell his face from his handkerchief at that distance; and this point remained undecided.

In the reaction that followed the feverish excitement of that day, Tennessee's Partner was not forgotten. A secret investigation had cleared him of any complicity in Tennessee's guilt, and left only a suspicion of his general sanity. Sandy Bar made a point of calling on him, and proffering various uncouth, but well-meant kindnesses. But from that day his rude health and great strength seemed visibly to decline; and when the rainy season fairly set in, and the tiny grass-blades were beginning to peep from the rocky mound above Tennessee's grave, he took to his bed.

One night, when the pines beside the cabin were swaying in the storm, and trailing their

slender fingers over the roof, and the roar and
rush of the swollen river were heard below, Tennessee's Partner lifted his head from the pillow,
saying, "It is time to go for Tennessee; I must
put 'Jinny' in the cart"; and would have risen
from his bed but for the restraint of his attendant.
Struggling, he still pursued his singular fancy:
"There, now, steady, 'Jinny,' — steady, old girl.
How dark it is! Look out for the ruts, — and look
out for him, too, old gal. Sometimes, you know,
when he's blind drunk, he drops down right in the
trail. Keep on straight up to the pine on the top
of the hill. Thar — I told you so! — thar he is,
— coming this way, too, — all by himself, sober,
and his face a-shining. Tennessee! Pardner!"

And so they met.

THE IDYL OF RED GULCH.

SANDY was very drunk. He was lying under an azalea-bush, in pretty much the same attitude in which he had fallen some hours before. How long he had been lying there he could not tell, and did n't care; how long he should lie there was a matter equally indefinite and unconsidered. A tranquil philosophy, born of his physical condition, suffused and saturated his moral being.

The spectacle of a drunken man, and of this drunken man in particular, was not, I grieve to say, of sufficient novelty in Red Gulch to attract attention. Earlier in the day some local satirist had erected a temporary tombstone at Sandy's head, bearing the inscription, "Effects of McCorkle's whiskey, — kills at forty rods," with a hand pointing to McCorkle's saloon. But this, I imagine, was, like most local satire, personal; and was a reflection upon the unfairness of the process rather than a commentary upon the impropriety of the result. With this facetious exception, Sandy had been undisturbed. A wandering mule, released from his pack, had cropped the scant herbage be-

side him, and sniffed curiously at the prostrate
man ; a vagabond dog, with that deep sympathy
which the species have for drunken men, had
licked his dusty boots, and curled himself up at
his feet, and lay there, blinking one eye in the
sunlight, with a simulation of dissipation that was
ingenious and dog-like in its implied flattery of
the unconscious man beside him.

Meanwhile the shadows of the pine-trees had
slowly swung around until they crossed the road,
and their trunks barred the open meadow with
gigantic parallels of black and yellow.   Little
puffs of red dust, lifted by the plunging hoofs of
passing teams, dispersed in a grimy shower upon
the recumbent man.   The sun sank lower and
lower ; and still Sandy stirred not.   And then the
repose of this philosopher was disturbed, as other
philosophers have been, by the intrusion of an
unphilosophical sex.

"Miss Mary," as she was known to the little
flock that she had just dismissed from the log
school-house beyond the pines, was taking her
afternoon walk.   Observing an unusually fine
cluster of blossoms on the azalea-bush opposite,
she crossed the road to pluck it, — picking her way
through the red dust, not without certain fierce little shivers of disgust, and some feline circumlocu-
tion.   And then she came suddenly upon Sandy !

Of course she uttered the little *staccato* cry of

her sex. But when she had paid that tribute to her physical weakness she became overbold, and halted for a moment, — at least six feet from this prostrate monster, — with her white skirts gathered in her hand, ready for flight. But neither sound nor motion came from the bush. With one little foot she then overturned the satirical head-board, and muttered " Beasts ! " — an epithet which probably, at that moment, conveniently classified in her mind the entire male population of Red Gulch. For Miss Mary, being possessed of certain rigid notions of her own, had not, perhaps, properly appreciated the demonstrative gallantry for which the Californian has been so justly celebrated by his brother Californians, and had, as a new-comer, perhaps, fairly earned the reputation of being " stuck up."

As she stood there she noticed, also, that the slant sunbeams were heating Sandy's head to what she judged to be an unhealthy temperature, and that his hat was lying uselessly at his side. To pick it up and to place it over his face was a work requiring some courage, particularly as his eyes were open. Yet she did it and made good her retreat. But she was somewhat concerned, on looking back, to see that the hat was removed, and that Sandy was sitting up and saying something.

The truth was, that in the calm depths of Sandy's mind he was satisfied that the rays of the sun were beneficial and healthful; that from childhood he had objected to lying down in a hat; that no people but condemned fools, past redemption, ever wore hats; and that his right to dispense with them when he pleased was inalienable. This was the statement of his inner consciousness. Unfortunately, its outward expression was vague, being limited to a repetition of the following formula, — " Su'shine all ri' ! Wasser maär, eh ? Wass up, su'shine ? "

Miss Mary stopped, and, taking fresh courage from her vantage of distance, asked him if there was anything that he wanted.

" Wass up ? Wasser maär ? " continued Sandy, in a very high key.

" Get up, you horrid man ! " said Miss Mary, now thoroughly incensed ; " get up, and go home."

Sandy staggered to his feet. He was six feet high, and Miss Mary trembled. He started forward a few paces and then stopped.

" Wass I go home for ? " he suddenly asked, with great gravity.

" Go and take a bath," replied Miss Mary, eying his grimy person with great disfavor.

To her infinite dismay, Sandy suddenly pulled off his coat and vest, threw them on the ground, kicked off his boots, and, plunging wildly forward, darted headlong over the hill, in the direction of the river.

"Goodness Heavens! — the man will be drowned!" said Miss Mary; and then, with feminine inconsistency, she ran back to the schoolhouse, and locked herself in.

That night, while seated at supper with her hostess, the blacksmith's wife, it came to Miss Mary to ask, demurely, if her husband ever got drunk. "Abner," responded Mrs. Stidger, reflectively, "let's see: Abner hasn't been tight since last 'lection." Miss Mary would have liked to ask if he preferred lying in the sun on these occasions, and if a cold bath would have hurt him; but this would have involved an explanation, which she did not then care to give. So she contented herself with opening her gray eyes widely at the red-cheeked Mrs. Stidger, — a fine specimen of Southwestern efflorescence, — and then dismissed the subject altogether. The next day she wrote to her dearest friend, in Boston: "I think I find the intoxicated portion of this community the least objectionable. I refer, my dear, to the men, of course. I do not know anything that could make the women tolerable."

In less than a week Miss Mary had forgotten this episode, except that her afternoon walks took thereafter, almost unconsciously, another direction. She noticed, however, that every morning a fresh cluster of azalea-blossoms appeared among the flowers on her desk. This was not

strange, as her little flock were aware of her fondness for flowers, and invariably kept her desk
bright with anemones, syringas, and lupines; but,
on questioning them, they, one and all, professed
ignorance of the azaleas. A few days later, Master Johnny Stidger, whose desk was nearest to
the window, was suddenly taken with spasms
of apparently gratuitous laughter, that threatened
the discipline of the school. All that Miss Mary
could get from him was, that some one had been
"looking in the winder." Irate and indignant, she
sallied from her hive to do battle with the intruder. As she turned the corner of the school-house
she came plump upon the quondam drunkard, —
now perfectly sober, and inexpressibly sheepish
and guilty-looking.

These facts Miss Mary was not slow to take a
feminine advantage of, in her present humor. But
it was somewhat confusing to observe, also, that
the beast, despite some faint signs of past dissipation, was amiable-looking, — in fact, a kind of
blond Samson, whose corn-colored, silken beard
apparently had never yet known the touch of bar-
ber's razor or Delilah's shears. So that the cut
ting speech which quivered on her ready tongue
died upon her lips, and she contented herself with
receiving his stammering apology with supercili-
ous eyelids and the gathered skirts of uncontam-
ination. When she re-entered the school-room,

her eyes fell upon the azaleas with a new sense of revelation. And then she laughed, and the little people all laughed, and they were all unconsciously very happy.

It was on a hot day — and not long after this — that two short-legged boys came to grief on the threshold of the school with a pail of water, which they had laboriously brought from the spring, and that Miss Mary compassionately seized the pail and started for the spring herself. At the foot of the hill a shadow crossed her path, and a blue-shirted arm dexterously, but gently relieved her of her burden. Miss Mary was both embarrassed and angry. "If you carried more of that for yourself," she said, spitefully, to the blue arm, without deigning to raise her lashes to its owner, "you'd do better." In the submissive silence that followed she regretted the speech, and thanked him so sweetly at the door that he stumbled. Which caused the children to laugh again, — a laugh in which Miss Mary joined, until the color came faintly into her pale cheek. The next day a barrel was mysteriously placed beside the door, and as mysteriously filled with fresh spring-water every morning.

Nor was this superior young person without other quiet attentions. "Profane Bill," driver of the Slumgullion Stage, widely known in the newspapers for his "gallantry" in invariably of-

fering the box-seat to the fair sex, had excepted
Miss Mary from this attention, on the ground that
he had a habit of " cussin' on up grades," and gave
her half the coach to herself. Jack Hamlin, a
gambler, having once silently ridden with her in
the same coach, afterward threw a decanter at the
head of a confederate for mentioning her name in
a bar-room. The over-dressed mother of a pupil
whose paternity was doubtful had often lingered
near this astute Vestal's temple, never daring to
enter its sacred precincts, but content to worship
the priestess from afar.

With such unconscious intervals the monotonous procession of blue skies, glittering sunshine,
brief twilights, and starlit nights passed over Red
Gulch. Miss Mary grew fond of walking in the
sedate and proper woods. Perhaps she believed,
with Mrs. Stidger, that the balsamic odors of the
firs " did her chest good," for certainly her slight
cough was less frequent and her step was firmer ;
perhaps she had learned the unending lesson which
the patient pines are never weary of repeating to
heedful or listless ears. And so, one day, she
planned a picnic on Buckeye Hill, and took the
children with her. Away from the dusty road,
the straggling shanties, the yellow ditches, the
clamor of restless engines, the cheap finery of shop-
windows, the deeper glitter of paint and colored
glass, and the thin veneering which barbarism

takes upon itself in such localities, — what infinite
relief was theirs! The last heap of ragged rock
and clay passed, the last unsightly chasm crossed,
— how the waiting woods opened their long
files to receive them! How the children — perhaps because they had not yet grown quite away
from the breast of the bounteous Mother — threw
themselves face downward on her brown bosom
with uncouth caresses, filling the air with their
laughter; and how Miss Mary herself — felinely
fastidious and intrenched as she was in the purity
of spotless skirts, collar, and cuffs — forgot all, and
ran like a crested quail at the head of her brood,
until, romping, laughing, and panting, with a
loosened braid of brown hair, a hat hanging by a
knotted ribbon from her throat, she came suddenly
and violently, in the heart of the forest, upon —
the luckless Sandy!

The explanations, apologies, and not overwise
conversation that ensued, need not be indicated
here. It would seem, however, that Miss Mary
had already established some acquaintance with
this ex-drunkard. Enough that he was soon accepted as one of the party; that the children, with
that quick intelligence which Providence gives the
helpless, recognized a friend, and played with his
blond beard, and long silken mustache, and took
other liberties, — as the helpless are apt to do.
And when he had built a fire against a tree, and

had shown them other mysteries of wood-craft, their admiration knew no bounds. At the close of two such foolish, idle, happy hours he found himself lying at the feet of the schoolmistress, gazing dreamily in her face, as she sat upon the sloping hillside, weaving wreaths of laurel and syringa, in very much the same attitude as he had lain when first they met. Nor was the similitude greatly forced. The weakness of an easy, sensuous nature, that had found a dreamy exaltation in liquor, it is to be feared was now finding an equal intoxication in love.

I think that Sandy was dimly conscious of this himself. I know that he longed to be doing something, — slaying a grizzly, scalping a savage, or sacrificing himself in some way for the sake of this sallow-faced, gray-eyed schoolmistress. As I should like to present him in a heroic attitude, I stay my hand with great difficulty at this moment, being only withheld from introducing such an episode by a strong conviction that it does not usually occur at such times. And I trust that my fairest reader, who remembers that, in a real crisis, it is always some uninteresting stranger or unromantic policeman, and not Adolphus, who rescues, will forgive the omission.

So they sat there, undisturbed, — the woodpeckers chattering overhead, and the voices of the children coming pleasantly from the hollow below.

What they said matters little. What they thought — which might have been interesting — did not transpire. The woodpeckers only learned how Miss Mary was an orphan; how she left her uncle's house, to come to California, for the sake of health and independence; how Sandy was an orphan, too; how he came to California for excitement; how he had lived a wild life, and how he was trying to reform; and other details, which, from a woodpecker's view-point, undoubtedly must have seemed stupid, and a waste of time. But even in such trifles was the afternoon spent; and when the children were again gathered, and Sandy, with a delicacy which the schoolmistress well understood, took leave of them quietly at the outskirts of the settlement, it had seemed the shortest day of her weary life.

As the long, dry summer withered to its roots, the school term of Red Gulch — to use a local euphuism — "dried up" also. In another day Miss Mary would be free; and for a season, at least, Red Gulch would know her no more. She was seated alone in the school-house, her cheek resting on her hand, her eyes half closed in one of those day-dreams in which Miss Mary — I fear, to the danger of school discipline — was lately in the habit of indulging. Her lap was full of mosses, ferns, and other woodland memories. She was so preoccupied with these and her own

thoughts that a gentle tapping at the door passed
unheard, or translated itself into the remembrance
of far-off woodpeckers. When at last it asserted
itself more distinctly, she started up with a flushed
cheek and opened the door. On the threshold
stood a woman, the self-assertion and audacity of
whose dress were in singular contrast to her timid,
irresolute bearing.

Miss Mary recognized at a glance the dubious
mother of her anonymous pupil. Perhaps she was
disappointed, perhaps she was only fastidious; but
as she coldly invited her to enter, she half unconsciously settled her white cuffs and collar, and
gathered closer her own chaste skirts. It was,
perhaps, for this reason that the embarrassed
stranger, after a moment's hesitation, left her gorgeous parasol open and sticking in the dust beside
the door, and then sat down at the farther end
of a long bench. Her voice was husky as she
began : —

"I heerd tell that you were goin' down to the
Bay to-morrow, and I could n't let you go until
I came to thank you for your kindness to my
Tommy."

Tommy, Miss Mary said, was a good boy, and
deserved more than the poor attention she could
give him.

"Thank you, miss ; thank ye !" cried the stranger, brightening even through the color which

Red Gulch knew facetiously as her "war paint," and striving, in her embarrassment, to drag the long bench nearer the schoolmistress. "I thank you, miss, for that! and if I am his mother, there ain't a sweeter, dearer, better boy lives than him. And if I ain't much as says it, thar ain't a sweeter, dearer, angeler teacher lives than he's got."

Miss Mary, sitting primly behind her desk, with a ruler over her shoulder, opened her gray eyes widely at this, but said nothing.

"It ain't for you to be complimented by the like of me, I know," she went on, hurriedly. "It ain't for me to be comin' here, in broad day, to do it, either; but I come to ask a favor, — not for me, miss, — not for me, but for the darling boy."

Encouraged by a look in the young schoolmistress's eye, and putting her lilac-gloved hands together, the fingers downward, between her knees, she went on, in a low voice: —

"You see, miss, there's no one the boy has any claim on but me, and I ain't the proper person to bring him up. I thought some, last year, of sending him away to 'Frisco to school, but when they talked of bringing a schoolma'am here, I waited till I saw you, and then I knew it was all right, and I could keep my boy a little longer. And O, miss, he loves you so much; and if you could hear him talk about you, in his pretty way, and if he could ask you what I ask you now, you could n't refuse him.

"It is natural," she went on, rapidly, in a voice that trembled strangely between pride and humility, — "it's natural that he should take to you, miss, for his father, when I first knew him, was a gentleman, — and the boy must forget me, sooner or later, — and so I ain't a goin' to cry about that. For I come to ask you to take my Tommy, — God bless him for the bestest, sweetest boy that lives, — to — to — take him with you."

She had risen and caught the young girl's hand in her own, and had fallen on her knees beside her.

"I've money plenty, and it's all yours and his. Put him in some good school, where you can go and see him, and help him to — to — to forget his mother. Do with him what you like. The worst you can do will be kindness to what he will learn with me. Only take him out of this wicked life, this cruel place, this home of shame and sorrow. You will; I know you will, — won't you? You will, — you must not, you cannot say no! You will make him as pure, as gentle as yourself; and when he has grown up, you will tell him his father's name, — the name that has n't passed my lips for years, — the name of Alexander Morton, whom they call here Sandy! Miss Mary! — do not take your hand away! Miss Mary, speak to me! You will take my boy? Do not put your

face from me. I know it ought not to look on such
as me. Miss Mary!—my God, be merciful!—
she is leaving me!"

Miss Mary had risen, and, in the gathering twilight, had felt her way to the open window. She
stood there, leaning against the casement, her eyes
fixed on the last rosy tints that were fading from
the western sky. There was still some of its light
on her pure young forehead, on her white collar,
on her clasped white hands, but all fading slowly
away. The suppliant had dragged herself, still on
her knees, beside her.

" I know it takes time to consider. I will wait
here all night; but I cannot go until you speak.
Do not deny me now. You will!—I see it in
your sweet face,— such a face as I have seen in
my dreams. I see it in your eyes, Miss Mary!—
you will take my boy!"

The last red beam crept higher, suffused Miss
Mary's eyes with something of its glory, flickered,
and faded, and went out. The sun had set on Red
Gulch. In the twilight and silence Miss Mary's
voice sounded pleasantly.

" I will take the boy. Send him to me to-
night."

The happy mother raised the hem of Miss Mary's skirts to her lips. She would have buried her
hot face in its virgin folds, but she dared not.
She rose to her feet.

" Does — this man — know of your intention ? "
asked Miss Mary, suddenly.

" No, nor cares.   He has never even seen the
child to know it."

" Go to him at once, — to-night, — now !   Tell
him what you have done.   Tell him I have taken
his child, and tell him — he must never see — see
— the child again.   Wherever it may be, he must
not come ; wherever I may take it, he must not
follow !   There, go now, please, — I 'm weary, and
— have much yet to do ! "

They walked together to the door.   On the
threshold the woman turned.

" Good night."

She would have fallen at Miss Mary's feet.   But
at the same moment the young girl reached out
her arms, caught the sinful woman to her own pure
breast for one brief moment, and then closed and
locked the door.

It was with a sudden sense of great responsibility that Profane Bill took the reins of the Slumgullion Stage the next morning, for the schoolmistress was one of his passengers.   As he entered the high-road, in obedience to a pleasant
voice from the " inside," he suddenly reined up
his horses and respectfully waited, as " Tommy "
hopped out at the command of Miss Mary.

" Not that bush, Tommy, — the next."

Tommy whipped out his new pocket-knife, and, cutting a branch from a tall azalea-bush, returned with it to Miss Mary.

" All right now ? "

" All right."

And the stage-door closed on the Idyl of Red Gulch.

BROWN OF CALAVERAS.

A SUBDUED tone of conversation, and the absence of cigar-smoke and boot-heels at the windows of the Wingdam stage-coach, made it evident that one of the inside passengers was a woman. A disposition on the part of loungers at the stations to congregate before the window, and some concern in regard to the appearance of coats, hats, and collars, further indicated that she was lovely. All of which Mr. Jack Hamlin, on the box-seat, noted with the smile of cynical philosophy. Not that he depreciated the sex, but that he recognized therein a deceitful element, the pursuit of which sometimes drew mankind away from the equally uncertain blandishments of poker, — of which it may be remarked that Mr. Hamlin was a professional exponent.

So that, when he placed his narrow boot on the wheel and leaped down, he did not even glance at the window from which a green veil was fluttering, but lounged up and down with that listless and grave indifference of his class, which was, perhaps, the next thing to good-breeding. With his closely buttoned figure and self-contained air he was a marked contrast to the other passengers, with their feverish restlessness, and boisterous emotion ; and even Bill Masters, a graduate of Harvard, with his slovenly dress, his overflowing vitality, his intense appreciation of lawlessness and barbarism, and his mouth filled with crackers and cheese, I fear cut but an unromantic figure beside this lonely calculator of chances, with his pale Greek face and Homeric gravity.

The driver called " All aboard !" and Mr. Hamlin returned to the coach. His foot was upon the wheel, and his face raised to the level of the open window, when, at the same moment, what appeared to him to be the finest eyes in the world suddenly met his. He quietly dropped down again, addressed a few words to one of the inside passengers, effected an exchange of seats, and as quietly took his place inside. Mr. Hamlin never allowed his philosophy to interfere with decisive and prompt action.

I fear that this irruption of Jack cast some restraint upon the other passengers, — particularly those who were making themselves most agreeable to the lady. One of them leaned forward, and apparently conveyed to her information regarding Mr. Hamlin's profession in a single epithet. Whether Mr. Hamlin heard it, or whether he recognized in the informant a distinguished jurist, from whom, but a few evenings before, he had won several thousand dollars, I cannot say. His colorless face betrayed no sign; his black eyes, quietly observant, glanced indifferently past the legal gentleman, and rested on the much more pleasing features of his neighbor. An Indian stoicism — said to be an inheritance from his maternal ancestor — stood him in good service, until the rolling wheels rattled upon the river-gravel at Scott's Ferry, and the stage drew up at the International Hotel for dinner. The legal gentleman and a member of Congress leaped out, and stood ready to assist the descending goddess, while Colonel Starbottle, of Siskiyou, took charge of her parasol and shawl. In this multiplicity of attention there was a momentary confusion and delay. Jack Hamlin quietly opened the *opposite* door of the coach, took the lady's hand, — with that decision and positiveness which a hesitating and undecided sex know how to admire, — and in an instant had dexterously and gracefully swung her to the ground, and again lifted her to the platform. An audible chuckle on the box, I fear, came from that other cynic, "Yuba Bill," the driver. "Look keerfully arter that baggage, Kernel," said the expressman, with affected concern, as he looked after Colonel Starbottle, gloomily bringing up the rear of the triumphant procession to the waiting-room.

Mr. Hamlin did not stay for dinner. His horse was already saddled, and awaiting him. He dashed over the ford, up the gravelly hill, and out into the dusty perspective of the Wingdam road, like one leaving an unpleasant fancy behind him. The inmates of dusty cabins by the roadside shaded their eyes with their hands, and looked after him, recognizing the man by his horse, and speculating what "was up with Comanche Jack." Yet much of this interest centred in the horse, in a community where the time made by "French Pete's" mare, in his run from the Sheriff of Calaveras, eclipsed all concern in the ultimate fate of that worthy.

The sweating flanks of his gray at length recalled him to himself. He checked his speed, and, turning into a by-road, sometimes used as a cut-off, trotted leisurely along, the reins hanging listlessly from his fingers. As he rode on, the character of the landscape changed, and became more pastoral. Openings in groves of pine and sycamore disclosed some rude attempts at cultivation, — a flowering vine trailed over the porch of one cabin, and a woman rocked her cradled babe under the roses of another. A little farther on Mr. Hamlin came upon some barelegged children, wading in the willowy creek, and so wrought upon them with a badinage peculiar to himself, that they were emboldened to climb up his horse's legs and over his saddle, until he was fain to develop an exaggerated ferocity of demeanor, and to escape, leaving behind some kisses and coin. And then, advancing deeper into the woods, where all signs of habitation failed, he began to sing, — uplifting a tenor so singularly sweet, and shaded by a pathos so subduing and tender, that I wot the robins and linnets stopped to listen. Mr. Hamlin's voice was not cultivated; the subject of his song was some sentimental lunacy, borrowed from the negro minstrels; but there thrilled through all some occult quality of tone and expression that was unspeakably touching. Indeed, it was a wonderful sight to see this sentimental blackleg, with a pack of cards in his pocket and a revolver at his back, sending his voice before him through the dim woods with a plaint about his "Nelly's grave," in a way that overflowed the eyes of the listener. A sparrow-hawk, fresh from his sixth victim, possibly recognizing in Mr. Hamlin a kindred spirit, stared at him in surprise, and was fain to confess the superiority of man. With a superior predatory capacity, *he* could n't sing.

But Mr. Hamlin presently found himself again on the high-road, and at his former pace. Ditches and banks of gravel, denuded hillsides, stumps, and decayed trunks of trees, took the place of woodland and ravine, and indicated his approach to civilization. Then a church-steeple came in sight, and he knew that he had reached home. In a few moments he was clattering down the

single narrow street, that lost itself in a chaotic
ruin of races, ditches, and tailings at the foot of
the hill, and dismounted before the gilded windows of the " Magnolia " saloon.   Passing through
the long bar-room, he pushed open a green-baize
door, entered a dark passage, opened another door
with a pass-key, and found himself in a dimly
lighted room, whose furniture, though elegant and
costly for the locality, showed signs of abuse.   The
inlaid centre-table was overlaid with stained disks
that were not contemplated in the original design.
The embroidered arm-chairs were discolored, and
the green velvet lounge, on which Mr. Hamlin
threw himself, was soiled at the foot with the red
soil of Wingdam.

Mr. Hamlin did not sing in his cage.   He lay
still, looking at a highly colored painting above
him, representing a young creature of opulent
charms.   It occurred to him then, for the first
time, that he had never seen exactly that kind
of a woman, and that, if he should, he would not,
probably, fall in love with her.   Perhaps he was
thinking of another style of beauty.   But just then
some one knocked at the door.   Without rising,
he pulled a cord that apparently shot back a bolt,
for the door swung open, and a man entered.

The new-comer was broad-shouldered and ro-
bust, — a vigor not borne out in the face, which,
though handsome, was singularly weak, and dis-

figured by dissipation. He appeared to be also under the influence of liquor, for he started on seeing Mr. Hamlin, and said, "I thought Kate was here"; stammered, and seemed confused and embarrassed.

Mr. Hamlin smiled the smile which he had before worn on the Wingdam coach, and sat up, quite refreshed and ready for business.

"You did n't come up on the stage," continued the new-comer, "did you?"

"No," replied Hamlin; "I left it at Scott's Ferry. It is n't due for half an hour yet. But how 's luck, Brown?"

"D—— bad," said Brown, his face suddenly assuming an expression of weak despair; "I 'm cleaned out again. Jack," he continued, in a whining tone, that formed a pitiable contrast to his bulky figure, "can't you help me with a hundred till to-morrow's clean-up? You see I 've got to send money home to the old woman, and — you 've won twenty times that amount from me."

The conclusion was, perhaps, not entirely logical, but Jack overlooked it, and handed the sum to his visitor. "The old woman business is about played out, Brown," he added, by way of commentary; "why don't you say you want to buck agin' faro? You know you ain't married!"

"Fact, sir," said Brown, with a sudden gravity,

as if the mere contact of the gold with the palm
of the hand had imparted some dignity to his
frame. "I've got a wife — a d—— good one,
too, if I do say it — in the States. It's three
year since I've seen her, and a year since I've
writ to her. When things is about straight, and
we get down to the lead, I'm going to send for
her."

"And Kate?" queried Mr. Hamlin, with his
previous smile.

Mr. Brown, of Calaveras, essayed an archness of
glance, to cover his confusion, which his weak face
and whiskey-muddled intellect but poorly carried
out, and said, —

"D—— it, Jack, a man must have a little liberty, you know. But come, what do you say to a
little game? Give us a show to double this hundred."

Jack Hamlin looked curiously at his fatuous
friend. Perhaps he knew that the man was pre-
destined to lose the money, and preferred that it
should flow back into his own coffers rather than
any other. He nodded his head, and drew his
chair toward the table. At the same moment
there came a rap upon the door.

"It's Kate," said Mr. Brown.

Mr. Hamlin shot back the bolt, and the door
opened. But, for the first time in his life, he staggered to his feet, utterly unnerved and abashed,

and for the first time in his life the hot blood crimsoned his colorless cheeks to his forehead. For before him stood the lady he had lifted from the Wingdam coach, whom Brown — dropping his cards with a hysterical laugh — greeted as

" My old woman, by thunder !"

They say that Mrs. Brown burst into tears, and reproaches of her husband. I saw her, in 1857, at Marysville, and disbelieve the story. And the Wingdam Chronicle, of the next week, under the head of " Touching Reunion," said : " One of those beautiful and touching incidents, peculiar to California life, occurred last week in our city. The wife of one of Wingdam's eminent pioneers, tired of the effete civilization of the East and its inhospitable climate, resolved to join her noble husband upon these golden shores. Without informing him of her intention, she undertook the long journey, and arrived last week. The joy of the husband may be easier imagined than described. The meeting is said to have been indescribably affecting. We trust her example may be followed."

Whether owing to Mrs. Brown's influence, or to some more successful speculations, Mr. Brown's financial fortune from that day steadily improved. He bought out his partners in the " Nip and Tuck " lead, with money which was said to have been won

at poker, a week or two after his wife's arrival, but
which rumor, adopting Mrs. Brown's theory that
Brown had forsworn the gaming-table, declared to
have been furnished by Mr. Jack Hamlin. He built
and furnished the "Wingdam House," which pretty
Mrs. Brown's great popularity kept overflowing
with guests. He was elected to the Assembly,
and gave largess to churches. A street in Wingdam was named in his honor.

Yet it was noted that in proportion as he waxed
wealthy and fortunate, he grew pale, thin, and
anxious. As his wife's popularity increased, he
became fretful and impatient. The most uxorious
of husbands, he was absurdly jealous. If he
did not interfere with his wife's social liberty, it
was because it was maliciously whispered that
his first and only attempt was met by an outburst
from Mrs. Brown that terrified him into silence.
Much of this kind of gossip came from those of
her own sex whom she had supplanted in the
chivalrous attentions of Wingdam, which, like
most popular chivalry, was devoted to an admiration of power, whether of masculine force or feminine beauty. It should be remembered, too, in
her extenuation, that, since her arrival, she had
been the unconscious priestess of a mythological
worship, perhaps not more ennobling to her womanhood than that which distinguished an older Greek
democracy. I think that Brown was dimly con-

scious of this. But his only confidant was Jack Hamlin, whose *infelix* reputation naturally precluded any open intimacy with the family, and whose visits were infrequent.

It was midsummer, and a moonlit night; and Mrs. Brown, very rosy, large-eyed, and pretty, sat upon the piazza, enjoying the fresh incense of the mountain breeze, and, it is to be feared, another incense which was not so fresh, nor quite as innocent. Beside her sat Colonel Starbottle and Judge Boompointer, and a later addition to her court, in the shape of a foreign tourist. She was in good spirits.

" What do you see down the road ? " inquired the gallant Colonel, who had been conscious, for the last few minutes, that Mrs. Brown's attention was diverted.

" Dust," said Mrs. Brown, with a sigh. " Only Sister Anne's ' flock of sheep.' "

The Colonel, whose literary recollections did not extend farther back than last week's paper, took a more practical view. " It ain't sheep," he continued ; " it 's a horseman. Judge, ain't that Jack Hamlin's gray ? "

But the Judge did n't know ; and, as Mrs. Brown suggested the air was growing too cold for further investigations, they retired to the parlor.

Mr. Brown was in the stable, where he generally retired after dinner. Perhaps it was to show his contempt for his wife's companions; perhaps, like other weak natures, he found pleasure in the exercise of absolute power over inferior animals. He had a certain gratification in the training of a chestnut mare, whom he could beat or caress as pleased him, which he could n't do with Mrs. Brown.   It was here that he recognized a certain gray horse which had just come in, and, looking a little farther on, found his rider.   Brown's greeting was cordial and hearty; Mr. Hamlin's somewhat restrained.   But at Brown's urgent request, he followed him up the back stairs to a narrow corridor, and thence to a small room looking out upon the stable-yard.   It was plainly furnished with a bed, a table, a few chairs, and a rack for guns and whips.

"This yer 's my home, Jack," said Brown, with a sigh, as he threw himself upon the bed, and motioned his companion to a chair.   "Her room 's t' other end of the hall.   It 's more 'n six months since we 've lived together, or met, except at meals. It 's mighty rough papers on the head of the house, ain't it ? " he said, with a forced laugh.   "But I 'm glad to see you, Jack, d—— glad," and he reached from the bed, and again shook the unresponsive hand of Jack Hamlin.

"I brought ye up here, for I did n't want to talk in the stable; though, for the matter of that, it 's all round town.   Don't strike a light.   We

can talk here in the moonshine. Put up your feet
on that winder, and sit here beside me. Thar's
whiskey in that jug."

Mr. Hamlin did not avail himself of the information. Brown, of Calaveras, turned his face to
the wall, and continued : —

"If I did n't love the woman, Jack, I would n't
mind. But it's loving her, and seeing her, day
arter day, goin' on at this rate, and no one to put
down the brake; that's what gits me! But I'm
glad to see ye, Jack, d—— glad."

In the darkness he groped about until he had
found and wrung his companion's hand again. He
would have detained it, but Jack slipped it into
the buttoned breast of his coat, and asked, listlessly, "How long has this been going on?"

"Ever since she came here; ever since the day
she walked into the Magnolia. I was a fool then;
Jack, I'm a fool now; but I did n't know how
much I loved her till then. An I she has n't been
the same woman since.

"But that ain't all, Jack; and it's what I
wanted to see you about, and I'm glad you've
come. It ain't that she does n't love me any
more; it ain't that she fools with every chap
that comes along, for, perhaps, I staked her love
and lost it, as I did everything else at the Magnolia; and, perhaps, foolin' is nateral to some
women, and thar ain't no great harm done, 'cept

to the fools.   But, Jack, I think, — I think she
loves somebody else.   Don't move, Jack; don't
move ; if your pistol hurts ye, take it off.

"It's been more 'n six months now that she's
seemed unhappy and lonesome, and kinder nervous
and scared like.   And sometimes I've ketched
her lookin' at me sort of timid and pitying.   And
she writes to somebody.   And for the last week
she's been gathering her own things, — trinkets,
and furbelows, and jew'lry, — and, Jack, I think
she's goin' off.   I could stand all but that.   To
have her steal away like a thief — "   He put his
face downward to the pillow, and for a few moments there was no sound but the ticking of a
clock on the mantel.   Mr. Hamlin lit a cigar.
and moved to the open window.   The moon no
longer shone into the room, and the bed and its
occupant were in shadow.   "What shall I do.
Jack ? " said the voice from the darkness.

The answer came promptly and clearly from the
window-side, — "Spot the man, and kill him on
sight."

"But, Jack ? "

"He's took the risk ! "

"But will that bring *her* back ? "

Jack did not reply, but moved from the window
towards the door.

"Don't go yet, Jack ; light the candle, and sit
by the table.   It's a comfort to see ye, if nothin'
else."

Jack hesitated, and then complied. He drew a pack of cards from his pocket and shuffled them, glancing at the bed. But Brown's face was turned to the wall. When Mr. Hamlin had shuffled the cards, he cut them, and dealt one card on the opposite side of the table and towards the bed, and another on his side of the table for himself. The first was a deuce; his own card, a king. He then shuffled and cut again. This time "dummy" had a queen, and himself a four-spot. Jack brightened up for the third deal. It brought his adversary a deuce, and himself a king again. "Two out of three," said Jack, audibly.

"What's that, Jack?" said Brown.

"Nothing."

Then Jack tried his hand with dice; but he always threw sixes, and his imaginary opponent aces. The force of habit is sometimes confusing.

Meanwhile, some magnetic influence in Mr. Hamlin's presence, or the anodyne of liquor, or both, brought surcease of sorrow, and Brown slept. Mr. Hamlin moved his chair to the window, and looked out on the town of Wingdam, now sleeping peacefully, — its harsh outlines softened and subdued, its glaring colors mellowed and sobered in the moonlight that flowed over all. In the hush he could hear the gurgling of water in the ditches, and the sighing of the pines beyond the hill.

Then he looked up at the firmament, and as ne did so a star shot across the twinkling field. Presently another, and then another. The phenomenon suggested to Mr. Hamlin a fresh augury. If in another fifteen minutes another star should fall — He sat there, watch in hand, for twice that time, but the phenomenon was not repeated.

The clock struck two, and Brown still slept. Mr. Hamlin approached the table, and took from his pocket a letter, which he read by the flickering candle-light. It contained only a single line, written in pencil, in a woman's hand, —

"Be at the corral, with the buggy, at three."

The sleeper moved uneasily, and then awoke. "Are you there, Jack?"

"Yes."

"Don't go yet. I dreamed just now, Jack, — dreamed of old times. I thought that Sue and me was being married agin, and that the parson, Jack, was — who do you think? — you!"

The gambler laughed, and seated himself on the bed, — the paper still in his hand.

"It's a good sign, ain't it?" queried Brown.

"I reckon. Say, old man, had n't you better get up?"

The "old man," thus affectionately appealed to, rose, with the assistance of Hamlin's outstretched hand.

"Smoke?"

Brown mechanically took the proffered cigar.

" Light ? "

Jack had twisted the letter into a spiral, lit it, and held it for his companion. He continued to hold it until it was consumed, and dropped the fragment — a fiery star — from the open window. He watched it as it fell, and then returned to his friend.

" Old man," he said, placing his hands upon Brown's shoulders, " in ten minutes I 'll be on the road, and gone like that spark. We won't see each other agin ; but, before I go, take a fool's advice : sell out all you 've got, take your wife with you, and quit the country. It ain't no place for you, nor her. Tell her she must go ; make her go, if she won't. Don't whine because you can't be a saint, and she ain't an angel. Be a man, — and treat her like a woman. Don't be a d—— fool. Good by."

He tore himself from Brown's grasp, and leaped down the stairs like a deer. At the stable-door he collared the half-sleeping hostler, and backed him against the wall. " Saddle my horse in two minutes, or I 'll — " The ellipsis was frightfully suggestive.

" The missis said you was to have the buggy," stammered the man.

" D——n the buggy !"

The horse was saddled as fast as the nervous

hands of the astounded hostler could manipulate buckle and strap.

"Is anything up, Mr. Hamlin?" said the man, who, like all his class, admired the *élan* of his fiery patron, and was really concerned in his welfare.

"Stand aside!"

The man fell back. With an oath, a bound, and clatter, Jack was into the road. In another moment, to the man's half-awakened eyes, he was but a moving cloud of dust in the distance, towards which a star just loosed from its brethren was trailing a stream of fire.

But early that morning the dwellers by the Wingdam turnpike, miles away, heard a voice, pure as a sky-lark's, singing afield. They who were asleep turned over on their rude couches to dream of youth and love and olden days. Hard-faced men and anxious gold-seekers, already at work, ceased their labors and leaned upon their picks, to listen to a romantic vagabond ambling away against the rosy sunrise.

HIGH-WATER MARK.

WHEN the tide was out on the Dedlow Marsh, its extended dreariness was patent. Its spongy, low-lying surface, sluggish, inky pools, and tortuous sloughs, twisting their slimy way, eel-like, toward the open bay, were all hard facts. So were the few green tussocks, with their scant blades, their amphibious flavor, and unpleasant dampness. And if you choose to indulge your fancy, — although the flat monotony of the Dedlow Marsh was not inspiring, — the wavy line of scattered drift gave an unpleasant consciousness of the spent waters, and made the dead certainty of the returning tide a gloomy reflection, which no present sunshine could dissipate. The greener meadow-land seemed oppressed with this idea, and made no positive attempt at vegetation until the work of reclamation should be complete. In the bitter fruit of the low cranberry-bushes one might fancy he detected a naturally sweet disposition curdled and soured by an injudicious course of too much regular cold water.

The vocal expression of the Dedlow Marsh was also melancholy and depressing. The sepulchral

boom of the bittern, the shriek of the curlew, the
scream of passing brent, the wrangling of quarrel-
some teal, the sharp, querulous protest of the
startled crane, and syllabled complaint of the
" killdeer" plover were beyond the power of written expression. Nor was the aspect of these
mournful fowls at all cheerful and inspiring. Certainly not the blue heron standing midleg deep
in the water, obviously catching cold in a reckless
disregard of wet feet and consequences ; nor the
mournful curlew, the dejected plover, or the low-
spirited snipe, who saw fit to join him in his
suicidal contemplation ; nor the impassive king-
fisher — an ornithological Marius — reviewing the
desolate expanse ; nor the black raven that went
to and fro over the face of the marsh continually, but evidently could n't make up his mind
whether the waters had subsided, and felt low-
spirited in the reflection that, after all this trouble,
he would n't be able to give a definite answer.
On the contrary, it was evident at a glance that
the dreary expanse of Dedlow Marsh told unpleasantly on the birds, and that the season of
migration was looked forward to with a feeling of
relief and satisfaction by the full-grown, and of
extravagant anticipation by the callow, brood. But
if Dedlow Marsh was cheerless at the slack of the
low tide, you should have seen it when the tide
was strong and full. When the damp air blew

chilly over the cold, glittering expanse, and came to the faces of those who looked seaward like another tide ; when a steel-like glint marked the low hollows and the sinuous line of slough ; when the great shell-incrusted trunks of fallen trees arose again, and went forth on their dreary, purposeless wanderings, drifting hither and thither, but getting no farther toward any goal at the falling tide or the day's decline than the cursed Hebrew in the legend ; when the glossy ducks swung silently, making neither ripple nor furrow on the shimmering surface ; when the fog came in with the tide and shut out the blue above, even as the green below had been obliterated ; when boatmen, lost in that fog, paddling about in a hopeless way, started at what seemed the brushing of mermen's fingers on the boat's keel, or shrank from the tufts of grass spreading around like the floating hair of a corpse, and knew by these signs that they were lost upon Dedlow Marsh, and must make a night of it, and a gloomy one at that, — then you might know something of Dedlow Marsh at high water.

Let me recall a story connected with this latter view which never failed to recur to my mind in my long gunning excursions upon Dedlow Marsh. Although the event was briefly recorded in the county paper, I had the story, in all its eloquent detail, from the lips of the principal actor. I cannot hope to catch the varying emphasis and pecu-

liar coloring of feminine delineation, for my nar-
rator was a woman; but I'll try to give at least
its substance.

She lived midway of the great slough of Dedlow Marsh and a good-sized river, which de-
bouched four miles beyond into an estuary formed
by the Pacific Ocean, on the long sandy peninsula which constituted the southwestern boundary
of a noble bay. The house in which she lived
was a small frame cabin raised from the marsh
a few feet by stout piles, and was three miles distant from the settlements upon the river. Her
husband was a logger, — a profitable business in
a county where the principal occupation was the
manufacture of lumber.

It was the season of early spring, when her husband left on the ebb of a high tide, with a raft of
logs for the usual transportation to the lower end
of the bay. As she stood by the door of the little cabin when the voyagers departed she noticed
a cold look in the southeastern sky, and she remembered hearing her husband say to his companions that they must endeavor to complete
their voyage before the coming of the southwesterly gale which he saw brewing. And that night
it began to storm and blow harder than she had
ever before experienced, and some great trees fell
in the forest by the river, and the house rocked
like her baby's cradle.

But however the storm might roar about the little cabin, she knew that one she trusted had driven bolt and bar with his own strong hand, and that had he feared for her he would not have left her. This, and her domestic duties, and the care of her little sickly baby, helped to keep her mind from dwelling on the weather, except, of course, to hope that he was safely harbored with the logs at Utopia in the dreary distance. But she noticed that day, when she went out to feed the chickens and look after the cow, that the tide was up to the little fence of their garden-patch, and the roar of the surf on the south beach, though miles away, she could hear distinctly. And she began to think that she would like to have some one to talk with about matters, and she believed that if it had not been so far and so stormy, and the trail so impassable, she would have taken the baby and have gone over to Ryckman's, her nearest neighbor. But then, you see, he might have returned in the storm, all wet, with no one to see to him; and it was a long exposure for baby, who was croupy and ailing.

But that night, she never could tell why, she did n't feel like sleeping or even lying down. The storm had somewhat abated, but she still "sat and sat," and even tried to read. I don't know whether it was a Bible or some profane magazine that this poor woman read, but most probably the latter, for the words all ran together and made such sad nonsense that she was forced at last to put the book down and turn to that dearer volume which lay before her in the cradle, with its white initial leaf as yet unsoiled, and try to look forward to its mysterious future. And, rocking the cradle, she thought of everything and everybody, but still was wide awake as ever.

It was nearly twelve o'clock when she at last laid down in her clothes. How long she slept she could not remember, but she awoke with a dreadful choking in her throat, and found herself standing, trembling all over, in the middle of the room, with her baby clasped to her breast, and she was "saying something." The baby cried and sobbed, and she walked up and down trying to hush it, when she heard a scratching at the door. She opened it fearfully, and was glad to see it was only old Pete, their dog, who crawled, dripping with water, into the room. She would like to have looked out, not in the faint hope of her husband's coming, but to see how things looked; but the wind shook the door so savagely that she could hardly hold it. Then she sat down a little while, and then walked up and down a little while, and then she lay down again a little while. Lying close by the wall of the little cabin, she thought she heard once or twice something scrape slowly

against the clapboards, like the scraping of branches.
Then there was a little gurgling sound, "like the
baby made when it was swallowing"; then something went "click-click" and "cluck-cluck," so
that she sat up in bed. When she did so she was
attracted by something else that seemed creeping
from the back door towards the centre of the room.
It was n't much wider than her little finger, but
soon it swelled to the width of her hand, and began spreading all over the floor. It was water.

She ran to the front door and threw it wide
open, and saw nothing but water. She ran to the
back door and threw it open, and saw nothing but
water. She ran to the side window, and, throwing
that open, she saw nothing but water. Then she
remembered hearing her husband once say that
there was no danger in the tide, for that fell regularly, and people could calculate on it, and that he
would rather live near the bay than the river,
whose banks might overflow at any time. But
was it the tide? So she ran again to the back
door, and threw out a stick of wood. It drifted
away towards the bay. She scooped up some of
the water and put it eagerly to her lips. It was
fresh and sweet. It was the river, and not the
tide!

It was then — O, God be praised for his goodness! she did neither faint nor fall; it was then —
blessed be the Saviour for it was his merciful

H

hand that touched and strengthened her in this awful moment — that fear dropped from her like a garment, and her trembling ceased. It was then and thereafter that she never lost her self-command, through all the trials of that gloomy night.

She drew the bedstead towards the middle of the room, and placed a table upon it and on that she put the cradle. The water on the floor was already over her ankles, and the house once or twice moved so perceptibly, and seemed to be racked so, that the closet doors all flew open. Then she heard the same rasping and thumping against the wall, and, looking out, saw that a large uprooted tree, which had lain near the road at the upper end of the pasture, had floated down to the house. Luckily its long roots dragged in the soil and kept it from moving as rapidly as the current, for had it struck the house in its full career, even the strong nails and bolts in the piles could not have withstood the shock. The hound had leaped upon its knotty surface, and crouched near the roots shivering and whining. A ray of hope flashed across her mind. She drew a heavy blanket from the bed, and, wrapping it about the babe, waded in the deepening waters to the door. As the tree swung again, broadside on, making the little cabin creak and tremble, she leaped on to its trunk. By God's mercy she succeeded in obtaining a footing on its slippery surface, and, twining an arm about its roots, she held in the other her moaning child. Then something cracked near the front porch, and the whole front of the house she had just quitted fell forward, — just as cattle fall on their knees before they lie down, — and at the same moment the great redwood-tree swung round and drifted away with its living cargo into the black night.

For all the excitement and danger, for all her soothing of her crying babe, for all the whistling of the wind, for all the uncertainty of her situation, she still turned to look at the deserted and water-swept cabin. She remembered even then, and she wonders how foolish she was to think of it at that time, that she wished she had put on another dress and the baby's best clothes; and she kept praying that the house would be spared so that he, when he returned, would have something to come to, and it would n't be quite so desolate, and — how could he ever know what had become of her and baby? And at the thought she grew sick and faint. But she had something else to do besides worrying, for whenever the long roots of her ark struck an obstacle, the whole trunk made half a revolution, and twice dipped her in the black water. The hound, who kept distracting her by running up and down the tree and howling, at last fell off at one of these collisions. He swam for some time beside her, and she tried to get the poor beast upon the tree, but he "acted silly" and wild, and at last she lost sight of him forever.   Then she and her baby were left alone.   The light which had burned for a few minutes in the deserted cabin was quenched suddenly.   She could not then tell whither she was drifting.   The outline of the white dunes on the peninsula showed dimly ahead, and she judged the tree was moving in a line with the river.   It must be about slack water, and she had probably reached the eddy formed by the confluence of the tide and the overflowing waters of the river.   Unless the tide fell soon, there was present danger of her drifting to its channel, and being carried out to sea or crushed in the floating drift.   That peril averted, if she were carried out on the ebb toward the bay, she might hope to strike one of the wooded promontories of the peninsula, and rest till daylight.   Sometimes she thought she heard voices and shouts from the river, and the bellowing of cattle and bleating of sheep.   Then again it was only the ringing in her ears and throbbing of her heart.   She found at about this time that she was so chilled and stiffened in her cramped position that she could scarcely move, and the baby cried so when she put it to her breast that she noticed the milk refused to flow ; and she was so frightened at that, that she put her head under her shawl, and for the first time cried bitterly.

When she raised her head again, the boom of the surf was behind her, and she knew that her ark had again swung round. She dipped up the water to cool her parched throat, and found that it was salt as her tears. There was a relief, though, for by this sign she knew that she was drifting with the tide. It was then the wind went down, and the great and awful silence oppressed her. There was scarcely a ripple against the furrowed sides of the great trunk on which she rested, and around her all was black gloom and quiet. She spoke to the baby just to hear herself speak, and to know that she had not lost her voice. She thought then, — it was queer, but she could not help thinking it, — how awful must have been the night when the great ship swung over the Asiatic peak, and the sounds of creation were blotted out from the world. She thought, too, of mariners clinging to spars, and of poor women who were lashed to rafts, and beaten to death by the cruel sea. She tried to thank God that she was thus spared, and lifted her eyes from the baby who had fallen into a fretful sleep. Suddenly, away to the southward, a great light lifted itself out of the gloom, and flashed and flickered, and flickered and flashed again. Her heart fluttered quickly against the baby's cold cheek. It was the lighthouse at the entrance of the bay. As she was yet wondering, the tree suddenly rolled a little, dragged a little, and then seemed to lie quiet and still. She put out her hand and the current gurgled against it. The tree was aground, and, by the position of the light and the noise of the surf, aground upon the Dedlow Marsh.

Had it not been for her baby, who was ailing and croupy, had it not been for the sudden drying up of that sensitive fountain, she would have felt safe and relieved. Perhaps it was this which tended to make all her impressions mournful and gloomy. As the tide rapidly fell, a great flock of black brent fluttered by her, screaming and crying. Then the plover flew up and piped mournfully, as they wheeled around the trunk, and at last fearlessly lit upon it like a gray cloud. Then the heron flew over and around her, shrieking and protesting, and at last dropped its gaunt legs only a few yards from her. But, strangest of all, a pretty white bird, larger than a dove, — like a pelican, but not a pelican, — circled around and around her. At last it lit upon a rootlet of the tree, quite over her shoulder. She put out her hand and stroked its beautiful white neck, and it never appeared to move. It stayed there so long that she thought she would lift up the baby to see it, and try to attract her attention. But when she did so, the child was so chilled and cold, and had such a blue look under the little lashes which it did n't raise at all, that she screamed aloud, and the bird flew away, and she fainted.

Well, that was the worst of it, and perhaps it was not so much, after all, to any but herself. For when she recovered her senses it was bright sunlight, and dead low water. There was a confused noise of guttural voices about her, and an old squaw, singing an Indian "hushaby," and rocking herself from side to side before a fire built on the marsh, before which she, the recovered wife and mother, lay weak and weary. Her first thought was for her baby, and she was about to speak, when a young squaw, who must have been a mother herself, fathomed her thought and brought her the "mowitch," pale but living, in such a queer little willow cradle all bound up, just like the squaw's own young one, that she laughed and cried together, and the young squaw and the old squaw showed their big white teeth and glinted their black eyes and said, "Plenty get well, skeena mowitch," "wagee man come plenty soon," and she could have kissed their brown faces in her joy. And then she found that they had been gathering berries on the marsh in their queer, comical baskets, and saw the skirt of her gown fluttering on the tree from afar, and the old squaw could n't resist the temptation of procuring a new garment, and came down and discovered the "wagee" woman and child. And of course she gave the garment to the old squaw, as you may imagine, and when *he* came at last and rushed up to her, looking about ten years older in his anxiety, she felt so faint again that they had to carry her to the canoe. For, you see, he knew nothing about the flood until he met the Indians at Utopia, and knew by the signs that the poor woman was his wife. And at the next high-tide he towed the tree away back home, although it was n't worth the trouble, and built another house, using the old tree for the foundation and props, and called it after her, "Mary's Ark!" But you may guess the next house was built above High-water mark. And that's all.

Not much, perhaps, considering the malevolent capacity of the Dedlow Marsh. But you must tramp over it at low water, or paddle over it at high tide, or get lost upon it once or twice in the fog, as I have, to understand properly Mary's adventure, or to appreciate duly the blessings of living beyond High-Water Mark.

A LONELY RIDE.

AS I stepped into the Slumgullion stage I saw
that it was a dark night, a lonely road, and
that I was the only passenger. Let me assure the
reader that I have no ulterior design in making
this assertion. A long course of light reading has
forewarned me what every experienced intelligence
must confidently look for from such a statement.
The story-teller who wilfully tempts Fate by such
obvious beginnings; who is to the expectant reader
in danger of being robbed or half murdered, or
frightened by an escaped lunatic, or introduced to
his lady-love for the first time, deserves to be detected. I am relieved to say that none of these
things occurred to me. The road from Wingdam
to Slumgullion knew no other banditti than the
regularly licensed hotel-keepers; lunatics had not
yet reached such depth of imbecility as to ride
of their own free-will in California stages; and my
Laura, amiable and long-suffering as she always is,
could not, I fear, have borne up against these depressing circumstances long enough to have made
the slightest impression on me.

I stood with my shawl and carpet-bag in hand,

gazing doubtingly on the vehicle. Even in the darkness the red dust of Wingdam was visible on its roof and sides, and the red slime of Slumgullion clung tenaciously to its wheels. I opened the door; the stage creaked uneasily, and in the gloomy abyss the swaying straps beckoned me, like ghostly hands, to come in now, and have my sufferings out at once.

I must not omit to mention the occurrence of a circumstance which struck me as appalling and mysterious. A lounger on the steps of the hotel, whom I had reason to suppose was not in any way connected with the stage company, gravely descended, and, walking toward the conveyance, tried the handle of the door, opened it, expectorated in the carriage, and returned to the hotel with a serious demeanor. Hardly had he resumed his position, when another individual, equally disinterested, impassively walked down the steps, proceeded to the back of the stage, lifted it, expectorated carefully on the axle, and returned slowly and pensively to the hotel. A third spectator wearily disengaged himself from one of the Ionic columns of the portico and walked to the box, remained for a moment in serious and expectorative contemplation of the boot, and then returned to his column. There was something so weird in this baptism that I grew quite nervous.

Perhaps I was out of spirits. A number of in-

finitesimal annoyances, winding up with the res-
olute persistency of the clerk at the stage-office
to enter my name misspelt on the way-bill, had
not predisposed me to cheerfulness. The inmates
of the Eureka House, from a social view-point,
were not attractive. There was the prevailing
opinion — so common to many honest people —
that a serious style of deportment and conduct
toward a stranger indicates high gentility and
elevated station. Obeying this principle, all hi-
larity ceased on my entrance to supper, and general remark merged into the safer and uncompro-
mising chronicle of several bad cases of diphtheria,
then epidemic at Wingdam. When I left the
dining-room, with an odd feeling that I had been
supping exclusively on mustard and tea-leaves, I
stopped a moment at the parlor door. A piano,
harmoniously related to the dinner-bell, tinkled re-
sponsive to a diffident and uncertain touch. On the
white wall the shadow of an old and sharp profile
was bending over several symmetrical and shadowy
curls. " I sez to Mariar, Mariar, sez I, ' Praise to the
face is open disgrace.' " I heard no more. Dreading
some susceptibility to sincere expression on the
subject of female loveliness, I walked away, check-
ing the compliment that otherwise might have
risen unbidden to my lips, and have brought
shame and sorrow to the household.

It was with the memory of these experiences

resting heavily upon me, that I stood hesitatingly before the stage door. The driver, about to mount, was for a moment illuminated by the open door of the hotel. He had the wearied look which was the distinguishing expression of Wingdam. Satisfied that I was properly way-billed and receipted for, he took no further notice of me. I looked longingly at the box-seat, but he did not respond to the appeal. I flung my carpet-bag into the chasm, dived recklessly after it, and — before I was fairly seated — with a great sigh, a creaking of unwilling springs, complaining bolts, and harshly expostulating axle, we moved away. Rather the hotel door slipped behind, the sound of the piano sank to rest, and the night and its shadows moved solemnly upon us.

To say it was dark expressed but faintly the pitchy obscurity that encompassed the vehicle. The roadside trees were scarcely distinguishable as deeper masses of shadow; I knew them only by the peculiar sodden odor that from time to time sluggishly flowed in at the open window as we rolled by. We proceeded slowly; so leisurely that, leaning from the carriage, I more than once detected the fragrant sigh of some astonished cow, whose ruminating repose upon the highway we had ruthlessly disturbed. But in the darkness our progress, more the guidance of some mysterious instinct than any apparent volition of our own, gave an indefinable charm of security to our journey, that a moment's hesitation or indecision on the part of the driver would have destroyed.

I had indulged a hope that in the empty vehicle I might obtain that rest so often denied me in its crowded condition. It was a weak delusion. When I stretched out my limbs it was only to find that the ordinary conveniences for making several people distinctly uncomfortable were distributed throughout my individual frame. At last, resting my arms on the straps, by dint of much gymnastic effort I became sufficiently composed to be aware of a more refined species of torture. The springs of the stage, rising and falling regularly, produced a rhythmical beat, which began to painfully absorb my attention. Slowly this thumping merged into a senseless echo of the mysterious female of the hotel parlor, and shaped itself into this awful and benumbing axiom,— " Praise-to-the-face-is-open-disgrace. Praise–to–the–face–is–open–disgrace." Inequalities of the road only quickened its utterance or drawled it to an exasperating length.

It was of no use to seriously consider the statement. It was of no use to except to it indignantly. It was of no use to recall the many instances where praise to the face had redounded to the everlasting honor of praiser and bepraised ; of no use to dwell sentimentally on modest genius and

courage lifted up and strengthened by open commendation; of no use to except to the mysterious
female, — to picture her as rearing a thin-blooded
generation on selfish and mechanically repeated
axioms, — all this failed to counteract the monotonous repetition of this sentence.   There was nothing to do but to give in, — and I was about to accept it weakly, as we too often treat other illusions
of darkness and necessity, for the time being, —
when I became aware of some other annoyance
that had been forcing itself upon me for the last
few moments.   How quiet the driver was!

Was there any driver?   Had I any reason to
suppose that he was not lying, gagged and bound
on the roadside, and the highwayman, with blackened face who did the thing so quietly, driving me
— whither?   The thing is perfectly feasible.   And
what is this fancy now being jolted out of me.   A
story?   It's of no use to keep it back, — particularly in this abysmal vehicle, and here it comes:
I am a Marquis, — a French Marquis; French, because the peerage is not so well known, and the
country is better adapted to romantic incident, —
a Marquis, because the democratic reader delights
in the nobility.   My name is something *ligny*.   I
am coming from Paris to my country-seat at St.
Germain.   It is a dark night, and I fall asleep and
tell my honest coachman, André, not to disturb me,
and dream of an angel.   The carriage at last stops

at the chateau. It is so dark that when I alight I do not recognize the face of the footman who holds the carriage door. But what of that ? — *peste !* I am heavy with sleep. The same obscurity also hides the old familiar indecencies of the statues on the terrace ; but there is a door, and it opens and shuts behind me smartly. Then I find myself in a trap, in the presence of the brigand who has quietly gagged poor André and conducted the carriage thither. There is nothing for me to do, as a gallant French Marquis, but to say, "*Parbleu !*" draw my rapier, and die valorously ! I am found a week or two after, outside a deserted *cabaret* near the barrier, with a hole through my ruffled linen and my pockets stripped. No ; on second thoughts, I am rescued, — rescued by the angel I have been dreaming of, who is the assumed daughter of the brigand, but the real daughter of an intimate friend.

Looking from the window again, in the vain hope of distinguishing the driver, I found my eyes were growing accustomed to the darkness. I could see the distant horizon, defined by India-inky woods, relieving a lighter sky. A few stars widely spaced in this picture glimmered sadly. I noticed again the infinite depth of patient sorrow in their serene faces ; and I hope that the Vandal who first applied the flippant "twinkle" to them may not be driven melancholy mad by their reproachful eyes.

I noticed again the mystic charm of space that imparts a sense of individual solitude to each integer of the densest constellation, involving the smallest star with immeasurable loneliness.　Something of this calm and solitude crept over me, and I dozed in my gloomy cavern.　When I awoke the full moon was rising.　Seen from my window, it had an indescribably unreal and theatrical effect.　It was the full moon of Norma,—that remarkable celestial phenomenon which rises so palpably to a hushed audience and a sublime *andante* chorus, until the *Casta Diva* is sung,—the "inconstant moon" that then and thereafter remains fixed in the heavens as though it were a part of the solar system inaugurated by Joshua.　Again the white-robed Druids filed past me, again I saw that improbable mistletoe cut from that impossible oak, and again cold chills ran down my back with the first strain of the recitative.　The thumping springs essayed to beat time, and the private-box-like obscurity of the vehicle lent a cheap enchantment to the view. But it was a vast improvement upon my past experience, and I hugged the fond delusion.

My fears for the driver were dissipated with the rising moon.　A familiar sound had assured me of his presence in the full possession of at least one of his most important functions.　Frequent and full expectoration convinced me that his lips were as yet not sealed by the gag of highwaymen, and soothed my anxious ear. With this load lifted from my mind, and assisted by the mild presence of Diana, who left, as when she visited Endymion, much of her splendor outside my cavern, — I looked around the empty vehicle. On the forward seat lay a woman's hair-pin. I picked it up with an interest that, however, soon abated. There was no scent of the roses to cling to it still, not even of hair-oil. No bend or twist in its rigid angles betrayed any trait of its wearer's character. I tried to think that it might have been "Mariar's." I tried to imagine that, confining the symmetrical curls of that girl, it might have heard the soft compliments whispered in her ears, which provoked the wrath of the aged female. But in vain. It was reticent and unswerving in its upright fidelity, and at last slipped listlessly through my fingers.

I had dozed repeatedly, — waked on the threshold of oblivion by contact with some of the angles of the coach, and feeling that I was unconsciously assuming, in imitation of a humble insect of my childish recollection, that spherical shape which could best resist those impressions, when I perceived that the moon, riding high in the heavens, had begun to separate the formless masses of the shadowy landscape. Trees isolated, in clumps and assemblages, changed places before my window. The sharp outlines of the distant

hills came back, as in daylight, but little softered
in the dry, cold, dewless air of a California summer night.   I was wondering how late it was, and
thinking that if the horses of the night travelled as
slowly as the team before us, Faustus might have
been spared his agonizing prayer, when a sudden
spasm of activity attacked my driver.   A succession of whip-snappings, like a pack of Chinese
crackers, broke from the box before me. The stage
leaped forward, and when I could pick myself
from under the seat, a long white building had in
some mysterious way rolled before my window.
It must be Slumgullion !   As I descended from the
stage I addressed the driver : —

   " I thought you changed horses on the road ? "
   " So we did.   Two hours ago."
   " That 's odd.   I did n't notice it."
   " Must have been asleep, sir.   Hope you had a
pleasant nap.   Bully place for a nice quiet snooze,
— empty stage, sir ! "

THE MAN OF NO ACCOUNT.

HIS name was Fagg,—David Fagg. He came to California in '52 with us, in the "Skyscraper." I don't think he did it in an adventurous way. He probably had no other place to go to. When a knot of us young fellows would recite what splendid opportunities we resigned to go, and how sorry our friends were to have us leave, and show daguerreotypes and locks of hair, and talk of Mary and Susan, the man of no account used to sit by and listen with a pained, mortified expression on his plain face, and say nothing. I think he had nothing to say. He had no associates except when we patronized him; and, in point of fact, he was a good deal of sport to us. He was always sea-sick whenever we had a capful of wind. He never got his sea-legs on either. And I never shall forget how we all laughed when Rattler took him the piece of pork on a string, and — But you know that time-honored joke. And then we had such a splendid lark with him. Miss Fanny Twinkler could n't bear the sight of him, and we used to make Fagg think that she had taken a

fancy to him, and send him little delicacies and
books from the cabin. You ought to have wit-
nessed the rich scene that took place when he
came up, stammering and very sick, to thank her!
Did n't she flash up grandly and beautifully and
scornfully? So like "Medora," Rattler said,—Rattler knew Byron by heart,—and was n't old Fagg
awfully cut up? But he got over it, and when
Rattler fell sick at Valparaiso, old Fagg used to
nurse him. You see he was a good sort of fellow,
but he lacked manliness and spirit.

He had absolutely no idea of poetry. I 've seen
him sit stolidly by, mending his old clothes, when
Rattler delivered that stirring apostrophe of Byron's to the ocean. He asked Rattler once, quite
seriously, if he thought Byron was ever sea-sick.
I don't remember Rattler's reply, but I know we
all laughed very much, and I have no doubt it was
something good, for Rattler was smart.

When the "Skyscraper" arrived at San Francisco we had a grand "feed." We agreed to meet
every year and perpetuate the occasion. Of course
we did n't invite Fagg. Fagg was a steerage-pas-
senger, and it was necessary, you see, now we were
ashore, to exercise a little discretion. But Old Fagg,
as we called him,—he was only about twenty-five
years old, by the way,—was the source of immense amusement to us that day. It appeared
that he had conceived the idea that he could walk

to Sacramento, and actually started off afoot. We had a good time, and shook hands with one another all around, and so parted. Ah me! only eight years ago, and yet some of those hands then clasped in amity have been clenched at each other, or have dipped furtively in one another's pockets. I know that we did n't dine together the next year, because young Barker swore he would n't put his feet under the same mahogany with such a very contemptible scoundrel as that Mixer; and Nibbles, who borrowed money at Valparaiso of young Stubbs, who was then a waiter in a restaurant, did n't like to meet such people.

When I bought a number of shares in the Coyote Tunnel at Mugginsville, in '54, I thought I'd take a run up there and see it. I stopped at the Empire Hotel, and after dinner I got a horse and rode round the town and out to the claim. One of those individuals whom newspaper correspondents call " our intelligent informant," and to whom in all small communities the right of answering questions is tacitly yielded, was quietly pointed out to me. Habit had enabled him to work and talk at the same time, and he never pretermitted either. He gave me a history of the claim, and added: "You see, stranger" (he addressed the bank before him), "gold is sure to come out 'er that theer claim (he put in a comma with his pick), but the old pro-pri-e-tor (he wriggled out the word and the point of his pick) warn't of much account (a long stroke of the pick for a period). He was green, and let the boys about here jump him,"— and the rest of his sentence was confided to his hat, which he had removed to wipe his manly brow with his red bandanna.

I asked him who was the original proprietor.

" His name war Fagg."

I went to see him. He looked a little older and plainer. He had worked hard, he said, and was getting on " so, so." I took quite a liking to him and patronized him to some extent. Whether I did so because I was beginning to have a distrust for such fellows as Rattler and Mixer is not necessary for me to state.

You remember how the Coyote Tunnel went in, and how awfully we shareholders were done! Well, the next thing I heard was that Rattler, who was one of the heaviest shareholders, was up at Mugginsville keeping bar for the proprietor of the Mugginsville Hotel, and that old Fagg had struck it rich, and did n't know what to do with his money. All this was told me by Mixer, who had been there, settling up matters, and likewise that Fagg was sweet upon the daughter of the proprietor of the aforesaid hotel. And so by hearsay and letter I eventually gathered that old Robins, the hotel man, was trying to get up a match between Nellie Robins and Fagg. Nellie was a pretty, plump, and foolish little thing, and would do just as her father wished. I thought it would be a good thing for Fagg if he should marry and settle down; that as a married man he might be of some account. So I ran up to Mugginsville one day to look after things.

It did me an immense deal of good to make Rattler mix my drinks for me, — Rattler! the gay, brilliant, and unconquerable Rattler, who had tried to snub me two years ago. I talked to him about old Fagg and Nellie, particularly as I thought the subject was distasteful. He never liked Fagg, and he was sure, he said, that Nellie did n't. Did Nellie like anybody else? He turned around to the mirror behind the bar and brushed up his hair! I understood the conceited wretch. I thought I'd put Fagg on his guard and get him to hurry up matters. I had a long talk with him. You could see by the way the poor fellow acted that he was badly stuck. He sighed, and promised to pluck up courage to hurry matters to a crisis. Nellie was a good girl, and I think had a sort of quiet respect for old Fagg's unobtrusiveness. But her fancy was already taken captive by Rattler's superficial qualities, which were obvious and pleasing. I don't think Nellie was any worse than you or I. We are more apt to take acquaintances at their apparent value than their intrinsic worth. It 's less trouble, and, except when we want to

trust them, quite as convenient. The difficulty
with women is that their feelings are apt to get
interested sooner than ours, and then, you know,
reasoning is out of the question. This is what old
Fagg would have known had he been of any account. But he was n't. So much the worse for
him.

It was a few months afterward, and I was sitting in my office when in walked old Fagg. I
was surprised to see him down, but we talked
over the current topics in that mechanical manner
of people who know that they have something
else to say, but are obliged to get at it in that formal way. After an interval Fagg in his natural
manner said, —

"I 'm going home !"

"Going home ?"

"Yes, — that is, I think I 'll take a trip to the
Atlantic States. I came to see you, as you know
I have some little property, and I have executed
a power of attorney for you to manage my affairs.
I have some papers I 'd like to leave with you.
Will you take charge of them ?"

"Yes," I said. "But what of Nellie ?"

His face fell. He tried to smile, and the com-
bination resulted in one of the most startling and
grotesque effects I ever beheld. At length he
said, —

"I shall not marry Nellie, — that is," — he

seemed to apologize internally for the positive form of expression, — " I think that I had better not."

"David Fagg," I said with sudden severity, "you're of no account ! "

To my astonishment his face brightened. "Yes," said he, "that's it ! — I'm of no account ! But I always knew it. You see I thought Rattler loved that girl as well as I did, and I knew she liked him better than she did me, and would be happier I dare say with him. But then I knew that old Robins would have preferred me to him, as I was better off, — and the girl would do as he said, — and, you see, I thought I was kinder in the way, — and so I left. But," he continued, as I was about to interrupt him, "for fear the old man might object to Rattler, I 've lent him enough to set him up in business for himself in Dogtown. A pushing, active, brilliant fellow, you know, like Rattler can get along, and will soon be in his old position again, — and you need n't be hard on him, you know, if he does n't. Good by."

I was too much disgusted with his treatment of that Rattler to be at all amiable, but as his business was profitable, I promised to attend to it, and he left. A few weeks passed. The return steamer arrived, and a terrible incident occupied the papers for days afterward. People in all parts of the State conned eagerly the details of an awful shipwreck, and those who had friends aboard went away by themselves, and read the long list of the lost under their breath. I read of the gifted, the gallant, the noble, and loved ones who had perished, and among them I think I was the first to read the name of David Fagg. For the "man of no account" had "gone home!"

STORIES.

MLISS.

CHAPTER I.

JUST where the Sierra Nevada begins to sub-
side in gentler undulations, and the rivers
grow less rapid and yellow, on the side of a
great red mountain, stands "Smith's Pocket."
Seen from the red road at sunset, in the red
light and the red dust, its white houses look like
the outcroppings of quartz on the mountain-side.
The red stage topped with red-shirted passengers
is lost to view half a dozen times in the tortuous
descent, turning up unexpectedly in out-of-the-
way places, and vanishing altogether within a
hundred yards of the town. It is probably owing
to this sudden twist in the road that the advent
of a stranger at Smith's Pocket is usually attended
with a peculiar circumstance. Dismounting from
the vehicle at the stage-office, the too confident
traveller is apt to walk straight out of town under
the impression that it lies in quite another direction. It is related that one of the tunnel-men,
two miles from town, met one of these self-

reliant passengers with a carpet-bag, umbrella,
Harper's Magazine, and other evidences of "Civilization and Refinement," plodding along over the
road he had just ridden, vainly endeavoring to
find the settlement of Smith's Pocket.

An observant traveller might have found some
compensation for his disappointment in the weird
aspect of that vicinity. There were huge fissures
on the hillside, and displacements of the red
soil, resembling more the chaos of some primary
elemental upheaval than the work of man; while,
half-way down, a long flume straddled its narrow
body and disproportionate legs over the chasm,
like an enormous fossil of some forgotten ante-
diluvian. At every step smaller ditches crossed
the road, hiding in their sallow depths unlovely
streams that crept away to a clandestine union
with the great yellow torrent below, and here and
there were the ruins of some cabin with the
chimney alone left intact and the hearthstone open
to the skies.

The settlement of Smith's Pocket owed its
origin to the finding of a " pocket " on its site
by a veritable Smith. Five thousand dollars
were taken out of it in one half-hour by Smith.
Three thousand dollars were expended by Smith
and others in erecting a flume and in tunnelling.
And then Smith's Pocket was found to be only
a pocket, and subject like other pockets to deple-

tion. Although Smith pierced the bowels of the great red mountain, that five thousand dollars was the first and last return of his labor. The mountain grew reticent of its golden secrets, and the flume steadily ebbed away the remainder of Smith's fortune. Then Smith went into quartz-mining; then into quartz-milling; then into hydraulics and ditching, and then by easy degrees into saloon-keeping. Presently it was whispered that Smith was drinking a great deal; then it was known that Smith was a habitual drunkard, and then people began to think, as they are apt to, that he had never been anything else. But the settlement of Smith's Pocket, like that of most discoveries, was happily not dependent on the fortune of its pioneer, and other parties projected tunnels and found pockets. So Smith's Pocket became a settlement with its two fancy stores, its two hotels, its one express-office, and its two first families. Occasionally its one long straggling street was overawed by the assumption of the latest San Francisco fashions, imported per express, exclusively to the first families; making outraged Nature, in the ragged outline of her furrowed surface, look still more homely, and putting personal insult on that greater portion of the population to whom the Sabbath, with a change of linen, brought merely the necessity of cleanliness, without the luxury of adornment. Then there was a Methodist Church, and hard by a Monte Bank, and a little beyond, on the mountain-side, a graveyard; and then a little school-house.

"The Master," as he was known to his little flock, sat alone one night in the school-house, with some open copy-books before him, carefully making those bold and full characters which are supposed to combine the extremes of chirographical and moral excellence, and had got as far as "Riches are deceitful," and was elaborating the noun with an insincerity of flourish that was quite in the spirit of his text, when he heard a gentle tapping. The woodpeckers had been busy about the roof during the day, and the noise did not disturb his work. But the opening of the door, and the tapping continuing from the inside, caused him to look up. He was slightly startled by the figure of a young girl, dirty and shabbily clad. Still, her great black eyes, her coarse, uncombed, lustreless black hair falling over her sun-burned face, her red arms and feet streaked with the red soil, were all familiar to him. It was Melissa Smith, — Smith's motherless child.

"What can she want here?" thought the master. Everybody knew "Mliss," as she was called, throughout the length and height of Red Mountain. Everybody knew her as an incorrigible girl. Her fierce, ungovernable disposition, her mad freaks and lawless character, were in their way as prover-

bial as the story of her father's weaknesses, and as
philosophically accepted by the townsfolk. She
wrangled with and fought the school-boys with
keener invective and quite as powerful arm. She
followed the trails with a woodman's craft, and the
master had met her before, miles away, shoeless,
stockingless, and bareheaded on the mountain
road. The miners' camps along the stream supplied her with subsistence during these voluntary
pilgrimages, in freely offered alms. Not but that
a larger protection had been previously extended
to Mliss. The Rev. Joshua McSnagley, "stated"
preacher, had placed her in the hotel as servant,
by way of preliminary refinement, and had introduced her to his scholars at Sunday school.
But she threw plates occasionally at the landlord,
and quickly retorted to the cheap witticisms of the
guests, and created in the Sabbath school a sensation that was so inimical to the orthodox dulness
and placidity of that institution, that, with a decent regard for the starched frocks and unblemished morals of the two pink-and-white-faced children of the first families, the reverend gentleman
had her ignominiously expelled. Such were the
antecedents, and such the character of Mliss, as she
stood before the master. It was shown in the
ragged dress, the unkempt hair, and bleeding feet,
and asked his pity. It flashed from her black,
fearless eyes, and commanded his respect.

7

" I come here to-night," she said rapidly and boldly, keeping her hard glance on his, " because I knew you was alone. I would n't come here when them gals was here. I hate 'em and they hates me. That 's why. You keep school, don't you ? I want to be teached ! "

If to the shabbiness of her apparel and uncomeliness of her tangled hair and dirty face she had added the humility of tears, the master would have extended to her the usual moiety of pity, and nothing more. But with the natural, though illogical instincts of his species, her boldness awakened in him something of that respect which all original natures pay unconsciously to one another in any grade. And he gazed at her the more fixedly as she went on still rapidly, her hand on that door-latch and her eyes on his : —

" My name 's Mliss, — Mliss Smith ! You can bet your life on that. My father 's Old Smith, — Old Bummer Smith, — that 's what 's the matter with him. Mliss Smith, — and I 'm coming to school ! "

" Well ? " said the master.

Accustomed to be thwarted and opposed, often wantonly and cruelly, for no other purpose than to excite the violent impulses of her nature, the master's phlegm evidently took her by surprise. She stopped ; she began to twist a lock of her hair between her fingers ; and the rigid line of upper lip, drawn over the wicked little teeth, relaxed and quivered slightly. Then her eyes dropped, and something like a blush struggled up to her cheek, and tried to assert itself through the splashes of redder soil, and the sunburn of years. Suddenly she threw herself forward, calling on God to strike her dead, and fell quite weak and helpless, with her face on the master's desk, crying and sobbing as if her heart would break.

The master lifted her gently and waited for the paroxysm to pass. When with face still averted, she was repeating between her sobs the *mea culpa* of childish penitence, — that " she 'd be good, she did n't mean to," etc., it came to him to ask her why she had left Sabbath school.

Why had she left the Sabbath school ? — why ? O yes. What did he (McSnagley) want to tell her she was wicked for ? What did he tell her that God hated her for ? If God hated her, what did she want to go to Sabbath school for ? *She* did n't want to be " beholden " to anybody who hated her.

Had she told McSnagley this ?

Yes, she had.

The master laughed. It was a hearty laugh, and echoed so oddly in the little school-house, and seemed so inconsistent and discordant with the sighing of the pines without, that he shortly corrected himself with a sigh. The sigh was quite as sincere in its way, however, and after a moment of serious silence he asked about her father.

Her father? What father? Whose father? What had he ever done for her? Why did the girls hate her? Come now! what made the folks say, " Old Bummer Smith's Mliss !" when she passed? Yes; O yes. She wished he was dead, — she was dead, — everybody was dead; and her sobs broke forth anew.

The master then, leaning over her, told her as well as he could what you or I might have said after hearing such unnatural theories from child‧ish lips; only bearing in mind perhaps better than you or I the unnatural facts of her ragged dress, her bleeding feet, and the omnipresent shadow of her drunken father. Then, raising her to her feet, he wrapped his shawl around her, and, bidding her come early in the morning, he walked with her down the road. There he bade her "good night." The moon shone brightly on the narrow path before them. He stood and watched the bent little figure as it staggered down the road, and waited until it had passed the little graveyard and reached the curve of the hill, where it turned and stood for a moment, a mere atom of suffering out-lined against the far-off patient stars. Then he went back to his work. But the lines of the copy-book thereafter faded into long parallels of never-ending road, over which childish figures seemed to pass sobbing and crying into the night. Then, the little school-house seeming lonelier than before, he shut the door and went home.

The next morning Mliss came to school. Her face had been washed, and her coarse black hair bore evidence of recent struggles with the comb, in which both had evidently suffered. The old defiant look shone occasionally in her eyes, but her manner was tamer and more subdued. Then began a series of little trials and self-sacrifices, in which master and pupil bore an equal part, and which increased the confidence and sympathy between them. Although obedient under the master's eye, at times during recess, if thwarted or stung by a fancied slight, Mliss would rage in ungovernable fury, and many a palpitating young savage, finding himself matched with his own weapons of torment, would seek the master with torn jacket and scratched face, and complaints of the dreadful Mliss. There was a serious division among the townspeople on the subject ; some threatening to withdraw their children from such evil companionship, and others as warmly upholding the course of the master in his work of reclamation. Meanwhile, with a steady persistence that seemed quite astonishing to him on looking back afterward, the master drew Mliss gradually out of the shadow of her past life, as though it were but her natural progress down the narrow

path on which he had set her feet the moonlit
night of their first meeting. Remembering the
experience of the evangelical McSnagley, he carefully avoided that Rock of Ages on which that
unskilful pilot had shipwrecked her young faith.
But if, in the course of her reading, she chanced
to stumble upon those few words which have lifted
such as she above the level of the older, the wiser,
and the more prudent, — if she learned something
of a faith that is symbolized by suffering, and the
old light softened in her eyes, it did not take
the shape of a lesson. A few of the plainer people
had made up a little sum by which the ragged
Mliss was enabled to assume the garments of respect and civilization; and often a rough shake of
the hand, and words of homely commendation from
a red-shirted and burly figure, sent a glow to the
cheek of the young master, and set him to thinking if it was altogether deserved.

Three months had passed from the time of their
first meeting, and the master was sitting late one
evening over the moral and sententious copies,
when there came a tap at the door, and again Mliss
stood before him. She was neatly clad and clean-
faced, and there was nothing perhaps but the long
black hair and bright black eyes to remind him of
his former apparition. " Are you busy ?" she
asked. " Can you come with me ?" — and on his
signifying his readiness, in her old wilful way she
said, " Come, then, quick !"

They passed out of the door together and into the dark road. As they entered the town the master asked her whither she was going. She replied, "To see my father."

It was the first time he had heard her call him by that filial title, or indeed anything more than "Old Smith" or the "Old Man." It was the first time in three months that she had spoken of him at all, and the master knew she had kept resolutely aloof from him since her great change. Satisfied from her manner that it was fruitless to question her purpose, he passively followed. In out-of-the-way places, low groggeries, restaurants, and saloons; in gambling-hells and dance-houses, the master, preceded by Mliss, came and went. In the reeking smoke and blasphemous outcries of low dens, the child, holding the master's hand, stood and anxiously gazed, seemingly unconscious of all in the one absorbing nature of her pursuit. Some of the revellers, recognizing Mliss, called to the child to sing and dance for them, and would have forced liquor upon her but for the interference of the master. Others, recognizing him mutely, made way for them to pass. So an hour slipped by. Then the child whispered in his ear that there was a cabin on the other side of the creek crossed by the long flume, where she thought he still might be. Thither they crossed, — a toilsome half-hour's walk, — but in vain. They were returning by the

ditch at the abutment of the flume, gazing at th
lights of the town on the opposite bank, when,
suddenly, sharply, a quick report rang out on the
clear night air. The echoes caught it, and carried
it round and round Red Mountain, and set the dogs
to barking all along the streams. Lights seemed
to dance and move quickly on the outskirts of the
town for a few moments, the stream rippled quite
audibly beside them, a few stones loosened themselves from the hillside and splashed into the
stream, a heavy wind seemed to surge the branches
of the funereal pines, and then the silence seemed
to fall thicker, heavier, and deadlier. The master
turned towards Mliss with an unconscious gesture
of protection, but the child had gone. Oppressed
by a strange fear, he ran quickly down the trail to
the river's bed, and, jumping from boulder to boulder, reached the base of Red Mountain and the
outskirts of the village. Midway of the crossing
he looked up and held his breath in awe. For
high above him on the narrow flume he saw the
fluttering little figure of his late companion crossing swiftly in the darkness.

He climbed the bank, and, guided by a few lights
moving about a central point on the mountain,
soon found himself breathless among a crowd of
awe-stricken and sorrowful men. Out from among
them the child appeared, and, taking the master's
hand, led him silently before what seemed a ragged

hole in the mountain. Her face was quite white, but her excited manner gone, and her look that of one to whom some long-expected event had at last happened, — an expression that to the master in his bewilderment seemed almost like relief. The walls of the cavern were partly propped by decaying timbers. The child pointed to what appeared to be some ragged, cast-off clothes left in the hole by the late occupant. The master approached nearer with his flaming dip, and bent over them. It was Smith, already cold, with a pistol in his hand and a bullet in his heart, lying beside his empty pocket.

CHAPTER II.

THE opinion which McSnagley expressed in reference to a "change of heart" supposed to be experienced by Mliss was more forcibly described in the gulches and tunnels. It was thought there that Mliss had "struck a good lead." So when there was a new grave added to the little enclosure, and at the expense of the master a little board and inscription put above it, the Red Mountain Banner came out quite handsomely, and did the fair thing to the memory of one of " our oldest Pioneers," alluding gracefully

7 *

to that "bane of noble intellects," and otherwise
genteelly shelving our dear brother with the past.
"He leaves an only child to mourn his loss," says
the Banner, "who is now an exemplary scholar,
thanks to the efforts of the Rev. Mr. McSnagley."
The Rev. McSnagley, in fact, made a strong point
of Mliss's conversion, and, indirectly attributing to
the unfortunate child the suicide of her father,
made affecting allusions in Sunday school to the
beneficial effects of the "silent tomb," and in this
cheerful contemplation drove most of the children
into speechless horror, and caused the pink-and-
white scions of the first families to howl dismally
and refuse to be comforted.

The long dry summer came.   As each fierce day
burned itself out in little whiffs of pearl-gray
smoke on the mountain summits, and the up-
springing breeze scattered its red embers over the
landscape, the green wave which in early spring
upheaved above Smith's grave grew sere and dry
and hard.   In those days the master, strolling in
the little churchyard of a Sabbath afternoon, was
sometimes surprised to find a few wild-flowers
plucked from the damp pine-forests scattered
there, and oftener rude wreaths hung upon the
little pine cross.   Most of these wreaths were
formed of a sweet-scented grass, which the children loved to keep in their desks, intertwined
with the plumes of the buckeye, the syringa,

and the wood-anemone, and here and there the
master noticed the dark blue cowl of the monk's-
hood, or deadly aconite. There was something
in the odd association of this noxious plant with
these memorials which occasioned a painful sensation to the master deeper than his esthetic sense.
One day, during a long walk, in crossing a wooded
ridge he came upon Mliss in the heart of the forest, perched upon a prostrate pine, on a fantastic
throne formed by the hanging plumes of lifeless
branches, her lap full of grasses and pine-burrs,
and crooning to herself one of the negro melodies
of her younger life. Recognizing him at a distance, she made room for him on her elevated
throne, and with a grave assumption of hospitality
and patronage that would have been ridiculous
had it not been so terribly earnest, she fed him
with pine-nuts and crab-apples. The master took
that opportunity to point out to her the noxious
and deadly qualities of the monk's-hood, whose
dark blossoms he saw in her lap, and extorted
from her a promise not to meddle with it as long
as she remained his pupil. This done, — as the
master had tested her integrity before, — he rested
satisfied, and the strange feeling which had overcome him on seeing them died away.

Of the homes that were offered Mliss when her
conversion became known, the master preferred
that of Mrs. Morpher, a womanly and kind-hearted

specimen of Southwestern efflorescence, known in
her maidenhood as the "Per-rairie Rose." Being
one of those who contend resolutely against their
own natures, Mrs. Morpher, by a long series of self-
sacrifices and struggles, had at last subjugated her
naturally careless disposition to principles of "order," which she considered, in common with Mr.
Pope, as "Heaven's first law." But she could not
entirely govern the orbits of her satellites, however
regular her own movements, and even her own
"Jeemes" sometimes collided with her. Again
her old nature asserted itself in her children. Ly-
curgus dipped into the cupboard "between meals,"
and Aristides came home from school without
shoes, leaving those important articles on the
threshold, for the delight of a barefooted walk
down the ditches. Octavia and Cassandra were
"keerless" of their clothes. So with but one exception, however much the "Prairie Rose" might
have trimmed and pruned and trained her own
matured luxuriance, the little shoots came up
defiantly wild and straggling. That one exception
was Clytemnestra Morpher, aged fifteen. She was
the realization of her mother's immaculate con-
ception, — neat, orderly, and dull.

It was an amiable weakness of Mrs. Morpher
to imagine that "Clytie" was a consolation and
model for Mliss. Following this fallacy, Mrs. Morpher threw Clytie at the head of Mliss when she

was "bad," and set her up before the child for adoration in her penitential moments. It was not, therefore, surprising to the master to hear that Clytie was coming to school, obviously as a favor to the master and as an example for Mliss and others. For "Clytie" was quite a young lady. Inheriting her mother's physical peculiarities, and in obedience to the climatic laws of the Red Mountain region, she was an early bloomer. The youth of Smith's Pocket, to whom this kind of flower was rare, sighed for her in April and languished in May. Enamored swains haunted the school-house at the hour of dismissal. A few were jealous of the master.

Perhaps it was this latter circumstance that opened the master's eyes to another. He could not help noticing that Clytie was romantic; that in school she required a great deal of attention; that her pens were uniformly bad and wanted fixing; that she usually accompanied the request with a certain expectation in her eye that was somewhat disproportionate to the quality of service she verbally required; that she sometimes allowed the curves of a round, plump white arm to rest on his when he was writing her copies; that she always blushed and flung back her blond curls when she did so. I don't remember whether I have stated that the master was a young man, — it's of little consequence, however; he had been severely educated in the school in which Clytie was taking her first lesson, and, on the whole, withstood the flexible curves and factitious glance like the fine young Spartan that he was. Perhaps an insufficient quality of food may have tended to this asceticism. He generally avoided Clytie; but one evening, when she returned to the school-house after something she had forgotten, and did not find it until the master walked home with her, I hear that he endeavored to make himself particularly agreeable, — partly from the fact, I imagine, that his conduct was adding gall and bitterness to the already overcharged hearts of Clytemnestra's admirers.

The morning after this affecting episode Mliss did not come to school. Noon came, but not Mliss. Questioning Clytie on the subject, it appeared that they had left the school together, but the wilful Mliss had taken another road. The afternoon brought her not. In the evening he called on Mrs. Morpher, whose motherly heart was really alarmed. Mr. Morpher had spent all day in search of her, without discovering a trace that might lead to her discovery. Aristides was summoned as a probable accomplice, but that equitable infant succeeded in impressing the household with his innocence. Mrs. Morpher entertained a vivid impression that the child would yet be found drowned in a ditch, or, what was almost as terrible, muddied and soiled beyond the redemption of soap and water. Sick at heart, the master returned to the school-house. As he lit his lamp and seated himself at his desk, he found a note lying before him addressed to himself, in Mliss's handwriting. It seemed to be written on a leaf torn from some old memorandum-book, and, to prevent sacrilegious trifling, had been sealed with six broken wafers. Opening it almost tenderly, the master read as follows : —

RESPECTED SIR, — When you read this, I am run away. Never to come back. *Never*, NEVER, NEVER. You can give my beeds to Mary Jennings, and my Amerika's Pride [a highly colored lithograph from a tobacco-box] to Sally Flanders. But don't you give anything to Clytie Morpher. Don't you dare to. Do you know what my oppinion is of her, it is this, she is perfekly disgustin. That is all and no more at present from

Yours respectfully,

MELISSA SMITH.

The master sat pondering on this strange epistle till the moon lifted its bright face above the distant hills, and illuminated the trail that led to the school-house, beaten quite hard with the coming and going of little feet. Then, more satisfied in mind, he tore the missive into fragments and scattered them along the road.

At sunrise the next morning he was picking his way through the palm-like fern and thick underbrush of the pine-forest, starting the hare from its form, and awakening a querulous protest from a few dissipated crows, who had evidently been making a night of it, and so came to the wooded ridge where he had once found Mliss. There he found the prostrate pine and tasselled branches, but the throne was vacant. As he drew nearer, what might have been some frightened animal started through the crackling limbs. It ran up the tossed arms of the fallen monarch, and sheltered itself in some friendly foliage. The master, reaching the old seat, found the nest still warm; looking up in the intertwining branches, he met the black eyes of the errant Mliss. They gazed at each other without speaking. She was first to break the silence.

" What do you want ? " she asked curtly.

The master had decided on a course of action. " I want some crab-apples," he said humbly.

"Sha' n't have 'em ! go away. Why don't you get 'em of Clytemnerestera ? " (It seemed to be a relief to Mliss to express her contempt in additional syllables to that classical young woman's already long-drawn title.) " O you wicked thing !"

" I am hungry, Lissy. I have eaten nothing since dinner yesterday. I am famished!" and the young man in a state of remarkable exhaustion leaned against the tree.

Melissa's heart was touched. In the bitter days of her gypsy life she had known the sensation he so artfully simulated. Overcome by his heart-broken tone, but not entirely divested of suspicion, she said, —

"Dig under the tree near the roots, and you'll find lots; but mind you don't tell," for Mliss had *her* hoards as well as the rats and squirrels.

But the master, of course, was unable to find them; the effects of hunger probably blinding his senses. Mliss grew uneasy. At length she peered at him through the leaves in an elfish way, and questioned, —

"If I come down and give you some, you'll promise you won't touch me?"

The master promised.

"Hope you'll die if you do!"

The master accepted instant dissolution as a forfeit. Mliss slid down the tree. For a few moments nothing transpired but the munching of the pine-nuts. "Do you feel better?" she asked, with some solicitude. The master confessed to a recuperated feeling, and then, gravely thanking her, proceeded to retrace his steps. As he expected, he had not gone far before she called him. He turned. She was standing there quite white, with tears in her widely opened orbs. The master felt that the right moment had come. Going up to her, he took both her hands, and, looking in her tearful eyes, said, gravely, "Lissy, do you remember the first evening you came to see me?"

Lissy remembered.

"You asked me if you might come to school, for you wanted to learn something and be better, and I said — "

"Come," responded the child, promptly.

"What would *you* say if the master now came to you and said that he was lonely without his little scholar, and that he wanted her to come and teach him to be better?"

The child hung her head for a few moments in silence. The master waited patiently. Tempted by the quiet, a hare ran close to the couple, and raising her bright eyes and velvet forepaws, sat and gazed at them. A squirrel ran half-way down the furrowed bark of the fallen tree, and there stopped.

"We are waiting, Lissy," said the master, in a whisper, and the child smiled. Stirred by a passing breeze, the tree-tops rocked, and a long pencil of light stole through their interlaced boughs full on the doubting face and irresolute little figure. Suddenly she took the master's hand in her quick way. What she said was scarcely audible, but the master, putting the black hair back from her forehead, kissed her; and so, hand in hand, they passed out of the damp aisles and forest odors into the open sunlit road.

CHAPTER III.

SOMEWHAT less spiteful in her intercourse with other scholars, Mliss still retained an offensive attitude in regard to Clytemnestra. Perhaps the jealous element was not entirely lulled in her passionate little breast. Perhaps it was only that the round curves and plump outline offered more extended pinching surface. But while such ebullitions were under the master's control, her enmity occasionally took a new and irrepressible form.

The master in his first estimate of the child's character could not conceive that she had ever possessed a doll. But the master, like many other professed readers of character, was safer in *a posteriori* than *a priori* reasoning. Mliss had a doll, but then it was emphatically Mliss's doll, — a smaller copy of herself. Its unhappy existence had been a secret discovered accidentally by Mrs. Morpher. It had been the old-time companion of Mliss's wanderings, and bore evident marks of suffering. Its original complexion was long since washed away by the weather and anointed by the slime of ditches. It looked very much as Mliss had in days past. Its one gown of faded stuff was dirty and ragged as hers had been. Mliss had never been known to apply to it any childish term of endearment. She never exhibited it in the presence of other children. It was put severely to bed in a hollow tree near the school-house, and only allowed exercise during Mliss's rambles. Fulfilling a stern duty to her doll, as she would to herself, it knew no luxuries.

Now Mrs. Morpher, obeying a commendable impulse, bought another doll and gave it to Mliss. The child received it gravely and curiously. The master on looking at it one day fancied he saw a slight resemblance in its round red cheeks and mild blue eyes to Clytemnestra. It became evident before long that Mliss had also noticed the same resemblance. Accordingly she hammered its waxen head on the rocks when she was alone, and sometimes dragged it with a string round its neck to and from school. At other times, setting it up on her desk, she made a pin-cushion of its patient and inoffensive body. Whether this was done in revenge of what she considered a second figurative obtrusion of Clytie's excellences upon her, or whether she had an intuitive appreciation of the rites of certain other heathens, and, indulging in that "Fetish" ceremony, imagined that the original of her wax model would pine away and finally die, is a metaphysical question I shall not now consider.

In spite of these moral vagaries, the master could not help noticing in her different tasks the

working of a quick, restless, and vigorous perception. She knew neither the hesitancy nor the
doubts of childhood. Her answers in class were
always slightly dashed with audacity. Of course
she was not infallible. But her courage and daring in passing beyond her own depth and that
of the floundering little swimmers around her, in
their minds outweighed all errors of judgment.
Children are not better than grown people in this
respect, I fancy; and whenever the little red hand
flashed above her desk, there was a wondering
silence, and even the master was sometimes oppressed with a doubt of his own experience and
judgment.

Nevertheless, certain attributes which at first
amused and entertained his fancy began to afflict
him with grave doubts. He could not but see that
Mliss was revengeful, irreverent, and wilful. That
there was but one better quality which pertained
to her semi-savage disposition, — the faculty of
physical fortitude and self-sacrifice, and another,
though not always an attribute of the noble savage,
— Truth. Mliss was both fearless and sincere;
perhaps in such a character the adjectives were
synonymous.

The master had been doing some hard thinking
on this subject, and had arrived at that conclusion
quite common to all who think sincerely, that he
was generally the slave of his own prejudices,

when he determined to call on the Rev. Mc-
Snagley for advice. This decision was somewhat
humiliating to his pride, as he and McSnagley were
not friends. But he thought of Mliss, and the
evening of their first meeting; and perhaps with
a pardonable superstition that it was not chance
alone that had guided her wilful feet to the school-
house, and perhaps with a complacent consciousness of the rare magnanimity of the act, he choked
back his dislike and went to McSnagley.

The reverend gentleman was glad to see him.
Moreover, he observed that the master was looking
" peartish," and hoped he had got over the " neu-
ralgy " and " rheumatiz." He himself had been
troubled with a dumb " ager " since last conference.
But he had learned to "rastle and pray."

Pausing a moment to enable the master to write
his certain method of curing the dumb "ager"
upon the book and volume of his brain, Mr. Mc-
Snagley proceeded to inquire after Sister Morpher.
" She is an adornment to Chris*tew*anity, and has a
likely growin' young family," added Mr. McSnagley; "and there's that mannerly young gal, — so
well behaved, — Miss Clytie." In fact, Clytie's
perfections seemed to affect him to such an extent
that he dwelt for several minutes upon them. The
master was doubly embarrassed. In the first place,
there was an enforced contrast with poor Mliss
in all this praise of Clytie. Secondly, there was

something unpleasantly confidential in his tone of
speaking of Mrs. Morpher's earliest born. So that
the master, after a few futile efforts to say something natural, found it convenient to recall another engagement, and left without asking the
information required, but in his after reflections
somewhat unjustly giving the Rev. Mr. McSnagley the full benefit of having refused it.

Perhaps this rebuff placed the master and pupil
once more in the close communion of old. The
child seemed to notice the change in the master's
manner, which had of late been constrained, and in
one of their long post-prandial walks she stopped
suddenly, and, mounting a stump, looked full in
his face with big, searching eyes. "You ain't mad?"
said she, with an interrogative shake of the black
braids. "No." "Nor bothered?" "No." "Nor
hungry?" (Hunger was to Mliss a sickness that
might attack a person at any moment.) "No."
"Nor thinking of her?" "Of whom, Lissy?"
"That white girl." (This was the latest epithet
invented by Mliss, who was a very dark brunette,
to express Clytemnestra.) "No." "Upon your
word?" (A substitute for "Hope you'll die!"
proposed by the master.) "Yes." "And sacred
honor?" "Yes." Then Mliss gave him a fierce
little kiss, and, hopping down, fluttered off. For
two or three days after that she condescended to
appear more like other children, and be, as she
expressed it, "good."

Two years had passed since the master's advent at Smith's Pocket, and as his salary was not large, and the prospects of Smith's Pocket eventually becoming the capital of the State not entirely definite, he contemplated a change. He had informed the school trustees privately of his intentions, but, educated young men of unblemished moral character being scarce at that time, he consented to continue his school term through the winter to early spring. None else knew of his intention except his one friend, a Dr. Duchesne, a young Creole physician known to the people of Wingdam as "Duchesny." He never mentioned it to Mrs. Morpher, Clytie, or any of his scholars. His reticence was partly the result of a constitutional indisposition to fuss, partly a desire to be spared the questions and surmises of vulgar curiosity, and partly that he never really believed he was going to do anything before it was done.

He did not like to think of Mliss. It was a selfish instinct, perhaps, which made him try to fancy his feeling for the child was foolish, romantic, and unpractical. He even tried to imagine that she would do better under the control of an older and sterner teacher. Then she was nearly eleven, and in a few years, by the rules of Red Mountain, would be a woman. He had done his duty. After Smith's death he addressed letters to Smith's relatives, and received one answer from a sister of Melissa's mother. Thanking the master, she stated her intention of leaving the Atlantic States for California with her husband in a few months. This was a slight superstructure for the airy castle which the master pictured for Mliss's home, but it was easy to fancy that some loving, sympathetic woman, with the claims of kindred, might better guide her wayward nature. Yet, when the master had read the letter, Mliss listened to it carelessly, received it submissively, and afterwards cut figures out of it with her scissors, supposed to represent Clytemnestra, labelled "the white girl," to prevent mistakes, and impaled them upon the outer walls of the school-house.

When the summer was about spent, and the last harvest had been gathered in the valleys, the master bethought him of gathering in a few ripened shoots of the young idea, and of having his Harvest-Home, or Examination. So the savans and professionals of Smith's Pocket were gathered to witness that time-honored custom of placing timid children in a constrained position, and bullying them as in a witness-box. As usual in such cases, the most audacious and self-possessed were the lucky recipients of the honors. The reader will imagine that in the present instance Mliss and Clytie were pre-eminent, and divided public attention; Mliss with her clearness of material perception and self-reliance, Clytie with her placid

self-esteem and saint-like correctness of deportment. The other little ones were timid and blun-
dering. Mliss's readiness and brilliancy, of course,
captivated the greatest number and provoked the
greatest applause. Mliss's antecedents had unconsciously awakened the strongest sympathies of a
class whose athletic forms were ranged against the
walls, or whose handsome bearded faces looked in
at the windows. But Mliss's popularity was over-
thrown by an unexpected circumstance.

McSnagley had invited himself, and had been
going through the pleasing entertainment of fright-
ening the more timid pupils by the vaguest and most
ambiguous questions delivered in an impressive funereal tone ; and Mliss had soared into Astronomy,
and was tracking the course of our spotted ball
through space, and keeping time with the music of
the spheres, and defining the tethered orbits of
the planets, when McSnagley impressively arose.
" Meelissy ! ye were speaking of the revolutions
of this yere yearth and the move-*ments* of the sun,
and I think ye said it had been a doing of it since
the creashun, eh ? " Mliss nodded a scornful affirm-
ative. " Well, war that the truth ? " said McSnagley, folding his arms. " Yes," said Mliss, shutting
up her little red lips tightly. The handsome outlines at the windows peered further in the school-
room, and a saintly Raphael-face, with blond beard
and soft blue eyes, belonging to the biggest scamp

in the diggings, turned toward the child and whispered, " Stick to it, Mliss !" The reverend gentleman heaved a deep sigh, and cast a compassionate
glance at the master, then at the children, and
then rested his look on Clytie. That young woman
softly elevated her round, white arm. Its seduc-
tive curves were enhanced by a gorgeous and mas-
sive specimen bracelet, the gift of one of her humblest worshippers, worn in honor of the occasion.
There was a momentary silence. Clytie's round
cheeks were very pink and soft. Clytie's big eyes
were very bright and blue. Clytie's low-necked
white book-muslin rested softly on Clytie's white,
plump shoulders. Clytie looked at the master, and
the master nodded. Then Clytie spoke softly : —

" Joshua commanded the sun to stand still, and
it obeyed him !" There was a low hum of applause in the school-room, a triumphant expression
on McSnagley's face, a grave shadow on the master's, and a comical look of disappointment reflected from the windows. Mliss skimmed rapidly
over her Astronomy, and then shut the book with
a loud snap. A groan burst from McSnagley, an
expression of astonishment from the school-room,
a yell from the windows, as Mliss brought her red
fist down on the desk, with the emphatic decla-
ration, —

" It 's a d—n lie. I don't believe it !"

CHAPTER IV.

THE long wet season had drawn near its close.
Signs of spring were visible in the swelling buds
and rushing torrents. The pine-forests exhaled
the fresher spicery. The azaleas were already bud-
ding, the Ceanothus getting ready its lilac livery
for spring. On the green upland which climbed
Red Mountain at its southern aspect the long
spike of the monk's-hood shot up from its broad-
leaved stool, and once more shook its dark-blue
bells. Again the billow above Smith's grave was
soft and green, its crest just tossed with the foam
of daisies and buttercups. The little graveyard
had gathered a few new dwellers in the past year,
and the mounds were placed two by two by the
little paling until they reached Smith's grave, and
there there was but one. General superstition
had shunned it, and the plot beside Smith was
vacant.

There had been several placards posted about
the town, intimating that, at a certain period, a
celebrated dramatic company would perform, for
a few days, a series of " side-splitting " and
" screaming farces " ; that, alternating pleasantly
with this, there would be some melodrama and a
grand divertisement, which would include singing,

dancing, etc. These announcements occasioned a great fluttering among the little folk, and were the theme of much excitement and great specu-lation among the master's scholars. The master had promised Mliss, to whom this sort of thing was sacred and rare, that she should go, and on that momentous evening the master and Mliss "assisted."

The performance was the prevalent style of heavy mediocrity; the melodrama was not bad enough to laugh at nor good enough to excite. But the master, turning wearily to the child, was astonished, and felt something like self-accusation in noticing the peculiar effect upon her excitable nature. The red blood flushed in her cheeks at each stroke of her panting little heart. Her small passionate lips were slightly parted to give vent to her hurried breath. Her widely opened lids threw up and arched her black eyebrows. She did not laugh at the dismal comicalities of the funny man, for Mliss seldom laughed. Nor was she dis-creetly affected to the delicate extremes of the corner of a white handkerchief, as was the tender-hearted "Clytie," who was talking with her "feller" and ogling the master at the same moment. But when the performance was over, and the green curtain fell on the little stage, Mliss drew a long deep breath, and turned to the master's grave face with a half-apologetic smile and wearied gesture.

Then she said, " Now take me home!" and dropped
the lids of her black eyes, as if to dwell once more
in fancy on the mimic stage.

On their way to Mrs. Morpher's the master
thought proper to ridicule the whole performance.
Now he should n't wonder if Mliss thought that
the young lady who acted so beautifully was
really in earnest, and in love with the gentleman
who wore such fine clothes. Well, if she were in
love with him it was a very unfortunate thing!
" Why?" said Mliss, with an upward sweep of the
drooping lid. " Oh! well, he could n't support his
wife at his present salary, and pay so much a week
for his fine clothes, and then they would n't receive as much wages if they were married as if
they were merely lovers, — that is," added the
master, " if they are not already married to somebody else; but I think the husband of the pretty
young countess takes the tickets at the door, or
pulls up the curtain, or snuffs the candles, or does
something equally refined and elegant. As to the
young man with nice clothes, which are really nice
now, and must cost at least two and a half or
three dollars, not to speak of that mantle of
red drugget which I happen to know the price of,
for I bought some of it for my room once, — as to
this young man, Lissy, he is a pretty good fellow,
and if he does drink occasionally, I don't think
people ought to take advantage of it and give him

black eyes and throw him in the mud. Do you ? I am sure he might owe me two dollars and a half a long time, before I would throw it up in his face, as the fellow did the other night at Wingdam."

Mliss had taken his hand in both of hers and was trying to look in his eyes, which the young man kept as resolutely averted. Mliss had a faint idea of irony, indulging herself sometimes in a species of sardonic humor, which was equally visible in her actions and her speech. But the young man continued in this strain until they had reached Mrs. Morpher's, and he had deposited Mliss in her maternal charge. Waiving the invitation of Mrs. Morpher to refreshment and rest, and shading his eyes with his hand to keep out the blue-eyed Clytemnestra's siren glances, he excused himself, and went home.

For two or three days after the advent of the dramatic company, Mliss was late at school, and the master's usual Friday afternoon ramble was for once omitted, owing to the absence of his trustworthy guide. As he was putting away his books and preparing to leave the school-house, a small voice piped at his side, " Please, sir ? " The master turned and there stood Aristides Morpher.

" Well, my little man," said the master, impatiently, " what is it ? quick !"

" Please, sir, me and ' Kerg ' thinks that Mliss is going to run away agin."

"What's that, sir?" said the master, with that unjust testiness with which we always receive disagreeable news.

"Why, sir, she don't stay home any more, and 'Kerg' and me see her talking with one of those actor fellers, and she's with him now; and please, sir, yesterday she told 'Kerg' and me she could make a speech as well as Miss Cellerstina Montmoressy, and she spouted right off by heart," and the little fellow paused in a collapsed condition.

"What actor?" asked the master.

"Him as wears the shiny hat. And hair. And gold pin. And gold chain," said the just Aristides, putting periods for commas to eke out his breath.

The master put on his gloves and hat, feeling an unpleasant tightness in his chest and thorax, and walked out in the road. Aristides trotted along by his side, endeavoring to keep pace with his short legs to the master's strides, when the master stopped suddenly, and Aristides bumped up against him. "Where were they talking?" asked the master, as if continuing the conversation.

"At the Arcade," said Aristides.

When they reached the main street the master paused. "Run down home," said he to the boy. "If Mliss is there, come to the Arcade and tell me. If she is n't there, stay home; run!" And off trotted the short-legged Aristides.

The Arcade was just across the way, — a long,

rambling building containing a bar-room, billiard-room, and restaurant. As the young man crossed the plaza he noticed that two or three of the passers-by turned and looked after him. He looked at his clothes, took out his handkerchief and wiped his face, before he entered the bar-room. It contained the usual number of loungers, who stared at him as he entered. One of them looked at him so fixedly and with such a strange expression that the master stopped and looked again, and then saw it was only his own reflection in a large mirror. This made the master think that perhaps he was a little excited, and so he took up a copy of the Red Mountain Banner from one of the tables, and tried to recover his composure by reading the column of advertise-ments.

He then walked through the bar-room, through the restaurant, and into the billiard-room. The child was not there. In the latter apartment a person was standing by one of the tables with a broad-brimmed glazed hat on his head. The master recognized him as the agent of the dramatic company ; he had taken a dislike to him at their first meeting, from the peculiar fashion of wearing his beard and hair. Satisfied that the object of his search was not there, he turned to the man with a glazed hat. He had noticed the master, but tried that common trick of unconsciousness, in which vulgar natures always fail. Balancing a billiard-

8 *   L

cue in his hand, he pretended to play with a ball
in the centre of the table. The master stood opposite to him until he raised his eyes ; when their
glances met, the master walked up to him.

He had intended to avoid a scene or quarrel, but
when he began to speak, something kept rising in
his throat and retarded his utterance, and his own
voice frightened him, it sounded so distant, low,
and resonant. "I understand," he began, "that
Melissa Smith, an orphan, and one of my scholars,
has talked with you about adopting your profession. Is that so ? "

The man with the glazed hat leaned over the
table, and made an imaginary shot, that sent the
ball spinning round the cushions. Then walking
round the table he recovered the ball and placed
it upon the spot. This duty discharged, getting
ready for another shot, he said, —

" S'pose she has ? "

The master choked up again, but, squeezing the
cushion of the table in his gloved hand, he went
on : —

" If you are a gentleman, I have only to tell you
that I am her guardian, and responsible for her career. You know as well as I do the kind of life
you offer her. As you may learn of any one here,
I have already brought her out of an existence
worse than death, — out of the streets and the con-
tamination of vice. I am trying to do so again.

Let us talk like men. She has neither father, mother, sister, or brother. Are you seeking to give her an equivalent for these?"

The man with the glazed hat examined the point of his cue, and then looked around for somebody to enjoy the joke with him.

"I know that she is a strange, wilful girl," continued the master, "but she is better than she was. I believe that I have some influence over her still. I beg and hope, therefore, that you will take no further steps in this matter, but as a man, as a gentleman, leave her to me. I am willing — " But here something rose again in the master's throat, and the sentence remained unfinished.

The man with the glazed hat, mistaking the master's silence, raised his head with a coarse, brutal laugh, and said in a loud voice, —

"Want her yourself, do you? That cock won't fight here, young man!"

The insult was more in the tone than the words, more in the glance than tone, and more in the man's instinctive nature than all these. The best appreciable rhetoric to this kind of animal is a blow. The master felt this, and, with his pent-up, nervous energy finding expression in the one act, he struck the brute full in his grinning face. The blow sent the glazed hat one way and the cue another, and tore the glove and skin from the master's hand from knuckle to joint. It opened

up the corners of the fellow's mouth, and spoilt
the peculiar shape of his beard for some time to
come.

There was a shout, an imprecation, a scuffle, and
the trampling of many feet. Then the crowd
parted right and left, and two sharp quick reports
followed each other in rapid succession. Then
they closed again about his opponent, and the master was standing alone. He remembered picking
bits of burning wadding from his coat-sleeve with
his left hand. Some one was holding his other
hand. Looking at it, he saw it was still bleeding
from the blow, but his fingers were clenched
around the handle of a glittering knife. He could
not remember when or how he got it.

The man who was holding his hand was Mr.
Morpher. He hurried the master to the door, but
the master held back, and tried to tell him as well
as he could with his parched throat about "Mliss."
"It's all right, my boy," said Mr. Morpher. "She's
home!" And they passed out into the street together. As they walked along Mr. Morpher said
that Mliss had come running into the house a few
moments before, and had dragged him out, saying
that somebody was trying to kill the master at the
Arcade. Wishing to be alone, the master promised Mr. Morpher that he would not seek the Agent
again that night, and parted from him, taking the
road toward the school-house. He was surprised

in nearing it to find the door open, — still more
surprised to find Mliss sitting there.

The master's nature, as I have hinted before,
had, like most sensitive organizations, a selfish
basis. The brutal taunt thrown out by his late
adversary still rankled in his heart. It was possible, he thought, that such a construction might
be put upon his affection for the child, which
at best was foolish and Quixotic. Besides, had
she not voluntarily abnegated his authority and
affection? And what had everybody else said
about her? Why should he alone combat the
opinion of all, and be at last obliged tacitly to
confess the truth of all they had predicted? And
he had been a participant in a low bar-room fight
with a common boor, and risked his life, to prove
what? What had he proved? Nothing? What
would the people say? What would his friends
say? What would McSnagley say?

In his self-accusation the last person he should
have wished to meet was Mliss. He entered the
door, and, going up to his desk, told the child, in a
few cold words, that he was busy, and wished to
be alone. As she rose he took her vacant seat, and,
sitting down, buried his head in his hands. When
he looked up again she was still standing there.
She was looking at his face with an anxious expression.

"Did you kill him?" she asked.

"No!" said the master.

"That's what I gave you the knife for!" said the child, quickly.

"Gave me the knife?" repeated the master, in bewilderment.

"Yes, gave you the knife. I was there under the bar. Saw you hit him. Saw you both fall. He dropped his old knife. I gave it to you. Why did n't you stick him?" said Mliss rapidly, with an expressive twinkle of the black eyes and a gesture of the little red hand.

The master could only look his astonishment.

"Yes," said Mliss. "If you'd asked me, I'd told you I was off with the play-actors. Why was I off with the play-actors? Because you would n't tell me you was going away. I knew it. I heard you tell the Doctor so. I was n't a goin' to stay here alone with those Morphers. I'd rather die first."

With a dramatic gesture which was perfectly consistent with her character, she drew from her bosom a few limp green leaves, and, holding them out at arm's-length, said in her quick vivid way, and in the queer pronunciation of her old life, which she fell into when unduly excited, —

"That's the poison plant you said would kill me. I'll go with the play-actors, or I'll eat this and die here. I don't care which. I won't stay here, where they hate and despise me! Neither would you let me, if you did n't hate and despise me too!"

The passionate little breast heaved, and two big tears peeped over the edge of Mliss's eyelids, but she whisked them away with the corner of her apron as if they had been wasps.

"If you lock me up in jail," said Mliss, fiercely, "to keep me from the play-actors, I'll poison myself. Father killed himself, — why should n't I? You said a mouthful of that root would kill me, and I always carry it here," and she struck her breast with her clenched fist.

The master thought of the vacant plot beside Smith's grave, and of the passionate little figure before him. Seizing her hands in his and looking full into her truthful eyes, he said, —

"Lissy, will you go with *me?*"

The child put her arms around his neck, and said joyfully, "Yes."

"But now — to-night?"

"To-night."

And, hand in hand, they passed into the road, — the narrow road that had once brought her weary feet to the master's door, and which it seemed she should not tread again alone. The stars glittered brightly above them. For good or ill the lesson had been learned, and behind them the school of Red Mountain closed upon them forever.

THE RIGHT EYE OF THE COMMANDER.

THE year of grace 1797 passed away on the coast of California in a southwesterly gale. The little bay of San Carlos, albeit sheltered by the headlands of the blessed Trinity, was rough and turbulent; its foam clung quivering to the seaward wall of the Mission garden; the air was filled with flying sand and spume, and as the Señor Comandante, Hermenegildo Salvatierra, looked from the deep embrasured window of the Presidio guard-room, he felt the salt breath of the distant sea buffet a color into his smoke-dried cheeks.

The Commander, I have said, was gazing thoughtfully from the window of the guard-room. He may have been reviewing the events of the year now about to pass away. But, like the garrison at the Presidio, there was little to review; the year, like its predecessors, had been uneventful, — the days had slipped by in a delicious monotony of simple duties, unbroken by incident or interruption. The regularly recurring feasts and saints' days, the half-yearly courier from San Diego, the rare transport-ship and rarer foreign

vessel, were the mere details of his patriarchal
life. If there was no achievement, there was certainly no failure. Abundant harvests and patient
industry amply supplied the wants of Presidio and
Mission. Isolated from the family of nations, the
wars which shook the world concerned them not
so much as the last earthquake; the struggle that
emancipated their sister colonies on the other side
of the continent to them had no suggestiveness.
In short, it was that glorious Indian summer of
California history, around which so much poetical
haze still lingers, — that bland, indolent autumn
of Spanish rule, so soon to be followed by the
wintry storms of Mexican independence and the
reviving spring of American conquest.

The Commander turned from the window and
walked toward the fire that burned brightly on
the deep oven-like hearth. A pile of copy-books,
the work of the Presidio school, lay on the table.
As he turned over the leaves with a paternal
interest, and surveyed the fair round Scripture
text, — the first pious pot-hooks of the pupils of
San Carlos, — an audible commentary fell from
his lips: "'Abimelech took her from Abraham'—
ah, little one, excellent! — 'Jacob sent to see his
brother' — body of Christ! that up-stroke of
thine, Paquita, is marvellous; the Governor shall
see it!" A film of honest pride dimmed the Commander's left eye, — the right, alas! twenty years

before had been sealed by an Indian arrow. He rubbed it softly with the sleeve of his leather jacket, and continued: "'The Ishmaelites having arrived —'"

He stopped, for there was a step in the courtyard, a foot upon the threshold, and a stranger entered. With the instinct of an old soldier, the Commander, after one glance at the intruder, turned quickly toward the wall, where his trusty Toledo hung, or should have been hanging. But it was not there, and as he recalled that the last time he had seen that weapon it was being ridden up and down the gallery by Pepito, the infant son of Bautista, the tortilio-maker, he blushed and then contented himself with frowning upon the intruder.

But the stranger's air, though irreverent, was decidedly peaceful. He was unarmed, and wore the ordinary cape of tarpauling and sea-boots of a mariner. Except a villanous smell of codfish, there was little about him that was peculiar.

His name, as he informed the Commander, in Spanish that was more fluent than elegant or precise, — his name was Peleg Scudder. He was master of the schooner "General Court," of the port of Salem, in Massachusetts, on a trading-voyage to the South Seas, but now driven by stress of weather into the bay of San Carlos. He begged permission to ride out the gale under the head-

lands of the blessed Trinity, and no more. Water
he did not need, having taken in a supply at
Bodega. He knew the strict surveillance of the
Spanish port regulations in regard to foreign vessels, and would do nothing against the severe discipline and good order of the settlement. There
was a slight tinge of sarcasm in his tone as he
glanced toward the desolate parade-ground of the
Presidio and the open unguarded gate. The fact
was that the sentry, Felipe Gomez, had discreetly
retired to shelter at the beginning of the storm,
and was then sound asleep in the corridor.

The Commander hesitated. The port regulations
were severe, but he was accustomed to exercise
individual authority, and beyond an old order
issued ten years before, regarding the American
ship " Columbia," there was no precedent to guide
him. The storm was severe, and a sentiment of
humanity urged him to grant the stranger's request.
It is but just to the Commander to say, that his
inability to enforce a refusal did not weigh with
his decision. He would have denied with equal
disregard of consequences that right to a seventy-
four gun ship which he now yielded so gracefully
to this Yankee trading-schooner. He stipulated
only, that there should be no communication
between the ship and shore. "For yourself,
Señor Captain," he continued, "accept my hospitality. The fort is yours as long as you shall

grace it with your distinguished presence"; and
with old-fashioned courtesy, he made the semblance
of withdrawing from the guard-room.

Master Peleg Scudder smiled as he thought of
the half-dismantled fort, the two mouldy brass
cannon, cast in Manila a century previous, and the
shiftless garrison.   A wild thought of accepting
the Commander's offer literally, conceived in the
reckless spirit of a man who never let slip an
offer for trade, for a moment filled his brain, but a
timely reflection of the commercial unimportance
of the transaction checked him.   He only took
a capacious quid of tobacco, as the Commander
gravely drew a settle before the fire, and in honor
of his guest untied the black silk handkerchief that
bound his grizzled brows.

What passed between Salvatierra and his guest
that night it becomes me not, as a grave chronicler
of the salient points of history, to relate.   I have
said that Master Peleg Scudder was a fluent talker,
and under the influence of divers strong waters,
furnished by his host, he became still more loqua-
cious.   And think of a man with a twenty years'
budget of gossip !   The Commander learned, for
the first time, how Great Britain lost her colonies ;
of the French Revolution ; of the great Napoleon,
whose achievements, perhaps, Peleg colored more
highly than the Commander's superiors would have
liked.   And when Peleg turned questioner, the

Commander was at his mercy. He gradually made himself master of the gossip of the Mission and Presidio, the "small-beer" chronicles of that pastoral age, the conversion of the heathen, the Presidio schools, and even asked the Commander how he had lost his eye! It is said that at this point of the conversation Master Peleg produced from about his person divers small trinkets, kick-shaws and new-fangled trifles, and even forced some of them upon his host. It is further alleged that under the malign influence of Peleg and several glasses of *aguardiente,* the Commander lost somewhat of his decorum, and behaved in a manner unseemly for one in his position, reciting high-flown Spanish poetry, and even piping in a thin, high voice, divers madrigals and heathen canzonets of an amorous complexion; chiefly in regard to a "little one" who was his, the Commander's, "soul"! These allegations, perhaps unworthy the notice of a serious chronicler, should be received with great caution, and are introduced here as simple hearsay. That the Commander, however, took a handkerchief and attempted to show his guest the mysteries of the *sembi cuacua,* capering in an agile but indecorous manner about the apartment, has been denied. Enough for the purposes of this narrative, that at midnight Peleg assisted his host to bed with many protestations of undying friendship, and then, as the gale had abated, took his leave of the Presidio and hurried aboard the " General Court." When the day broke the ship was gone.

I know not if Peleg kept his word with his host. It is said that the holy fathers at the Mission that night heard a loud chanting in the plaza, as of the heathens singing psalms through their noses; that for many days after an odor of salt codfish prevailed in the settlement; that a dozen hard nutmegs, which were unfit for spice or seed, were found in the possession of the wife of the baker, and that several bushels of shoe-pegs, which bore a pleasing resemblance to oats, but were quite inadequate to the purposes of provender, were discovered in the stable of the blacksmith. But when the reader reflects upon the sacredness of a Yankee trader's word, the stringent discipline of the Spanish port regulations, and the proverbial indisposition of my countrymen to impose upon the confidence of a simple people, he will at once reject this part of the story.

A roll of drums, ushering in the year 1798, awoke the Commander. The sun was shining brightly, and the storm had ceased. He sat up in bed, and through the force of habit rubbed his left eye. As the remembrance of the previous night came back to him, he jumped from his couch and ran to the window. There was no ship in the

day. A sudden thought seemed to strike him, and
he rubbed both of his eyes. Not content with
this, he consulted the metallic mirror which hung
beside his crucifix. There was no mistake ; the
Commander had a visible second eye, — a right
one, — as good, save for the purposes of vision, as
the left.

Whatever might have been the true secret of this
transformation, but one opinion prevailed at San
Carlos. It was one of those rare miracles vouch-
safed a pious Catholic community as an evidence
to the heathen, through the intercession of the
blessed San Carlos himself. That their beloved
Commander, the temporal defender of the Faith,
should be the recipient of this miraculous mani-
festation was most fit and seemly. The Commander himself was reticent ; he could not tell a
falsehood, — he dared not tell the truth. After all,
if the good folk of San Carlos believed that the
powers of his right eye were actually restored,
was it wise and discreet for him to undeceive
them ? For the first time in his life the Commander thought of policy, — for the first time he
quoted that text which has been the lure of so
many well-meaning but easy Christians, of being
" all things to all men." Infeliz Hermenegildo
Salvatierra !

For by degrees an ominous whisper crept through
the little settlement. The Right Eye of the Com-

mander, although miraculous, seemed to exercise a
baleful effect upon the beholder. No one could
look at it without winking. It was cold, hard,
relentless and unflinching. More than that, it
seemed to be endowed with a dreadful prescience,
— a faculty of seeing through and into the inarticu-
late thoughts of those it looked upon. The sol-
diers of the garrison obeyed the eye rather than
the voice of their commander, and answered his
glance rather than his lips in questioning. The
servants could not evade the ever-watchful, but
cold attention that seemed to pursue them. The
children of the Presidio School smirched their
copy-books under the awful supervision, and poor
Paquita, the prize pupil, failed utterly in that
marvellous up-stroke when her patron stood beside
her. Gradually distrust, suspicion, self-accusation,
and timidity took the place of trust, confidence,
and security throughout San Carlos. Whenever the
Right Eye of the Commander fell, a shadow fell
with it.

Nor was Salvatierra entirely free from the baleful influence of his miraculous acquisition. Unconscious of its effect upon others, he only saw in
their actions evidence of certain things that the
crafty Peleg had hinted on that eventful New
Year's eve. His most trusty retainers stammered,
blushed, and faltered before him. Self-accusations,
confessions of minor faults and delinquencies, or

extravagant excuses and apologies met his mildest
inquiries. The very children that he loved — his
pet pupil, Paquita — seemed to be conscious of
some hidden sin. The result of this constant ir-
ritation showed itself more plainly. For the first
half-year the Commander's voice and eye were at
variance. He was still kind, tender, and thoughtful in speech. Gradually, however, his voice took
upon itself the hardness of his glance and its
sceptical, impassive quality, and as the year again
neared its close it was plain that the Commander
had fitted himself to the eye, and not the eye to
the Commander.

It may be surmised that these changes did not
escape the watchful solicitude of the Fathers. Indeed, the few who were first to ascribe the right
eye of Salvatierra to miraculous origin and the
special grace of the blessed San Carlos, now talked
openly of witchcraft and the agency of Luzbel,
the evil one. It would have fared ill with Hermenegildo Salvatierra had he been aught but Commander or amenable to local authority. But the
reverend father, Friar Manuel de Cortes, had no
power over the political executive, and all attempts
at spiritual advice failed signally. He retired baf-
fled and confused from his first interview with the
Commander, who seemed now to take a grim satisfaction in the fateful power of his glance. The
holy father contradicted himself, exposed the fal-

9   M

lacies of his own arguments, and even, it is asserted, committed himself to several undoubted heresies. When the Commander stood up at mass, if the officiating priest caught that sceptical and searching eye, the service was inevitably ruined. Even the power of the Holy Church seemed to be lost, and the last hold upon the affections of the people and the good order of the settlement departed from San Carlos.

As the long dry summer passed, the low hills that surrounded the white walls of the Presidio grew more and more to resemble in hue the leathern jacket of the Commander, and Nature herself seemed to have borrowed his dry, hard glare. The earth was cracked and seamed with drought; a blight had fallen upon the orchards and vineyards, and the rain, long delayed and ardently prayed for, came not. The sky was as tearless as the right eye of the Commander. Murmurs of discontent, insubordination, and plotting among the Indians reached his ears; he only set his teeth the more firmly, tightened the knot of his black silk handkerchief, and looked up his Toledo.

The last day of the year 1798 found the Commander sitting, at the hour of evening prayers, alone in the guard-room. He no longer attended the services of the Holy Church, but crept away at such times to some solitary spot, where he spent the interval in silent meditation. The firelight played upon the low beams and rafters, but left the bowed figure of Salvatierra in darkness. Sitting thus, he felt a small hand touch his arm, and, looking down, saw the figure of Paquita, his little Indian pupil, at his knee. "Ah, littlest of all," said the Commander, with something of his old tenderness, lingering over the endearing diminutives of his native speech, — "sweet one, what doest thou here? Art thou not afraid of him whom every one shuns and fears?"

"No," said the little Indian, readily, "not in the dark. I hear your voice, — the old voice; I feel your touch, — the old touch; but I see not your eye, Señor Comandante. That only I fear, — and that, O Señor, O my father," said the child, lifting her little arms towards his, — "that I know is not thine own!"

The Commander shuddered and turned away. Then, recovering himself, he kissed Paquita gravely on the forehead and bade her retire. A few hours later, when silence had fallen upon the Presidio, he sought his own couch and slept peacefully.

At about the middle watch of the night a dusky figure crept through the low embrasure of the Commander's apartment. Other figures were flitting through the parade-ground, which the Commander might have seen had he not slept so quietly. The intruder stepped noiselessly to the couch and listened to the sleeper's deep-drawn inspiration. Something glittered in the firelight as the savage lifted his arm ; another moment and the sore perplexities of Hermenegildo Salvatierra would have been over, when suddenly the savage started and fell back in a paroxysm of terror. The Commander slept peacefully, but his right eye, widely opened, fixed and unaltered, glared coldly on the would-be assassin. The man fell to the earth in a fit, and the noise awoke the sleeper.

To rise to his feet, grasp his sword, and deal blows thick and fast upon the mutinous savages who now thronged the room, was the work of a moment. Help opportunely arrived, and the undisciplined Indians were speedily driven beyond the walls, but in the scuffle the Commander received a blow upon his right eye, and, lifting his hand to that mysterious organ, it was gone. Never again was it found, and never again, for bale or bliss, did it adorn the right orbit of the Commander.

With it passed away the spell that had fallen upon San Carlos. The rain returned to invigorate the languid soil, harmony was restored between priest and soldier, the green grass presently waved over the sere hillsides, the children flocked again to the side of their martial preceptor, a *Te Deum* was sung in the Mission Church, and pastoral content once more smiled upon the gentle valleys of

San Carlos. And far southward crept the "General Court" with its master, Peleg Scudder, trafficking in beads and peltries with the Indians, and offering glass eyes, wooden legs, and other Boston notions to the chiefs.

NOTES BY FLOOD AND FIELD.

PART I. — IN THE FIELD.

IT was near the close of an October day that I began to be disagreeably conscious of the Sacramento Valley. I had been riding since sunrise, and my course through the depressing monotony of the long level landscape affected me more like a dull dyspeptic dream than a business journey, performed under that sincerest of natural phenomena, — a California sky. The recurring stretches of brown and baked fields, the gaping fissures in the dusty trail, the hard outline of the distant hills, and the herds of slowly moving cattle, seemed like features of some glittering stereoscopic picture that never changed. Active exercise might have removed this feeling, but my horse by some subtle instinct had long since given up all ambitious effort, and had lapsed into a dogged trot.

It was autumn, but not the season suggested to the Atlantic reader under that title. The sharply defined boundaries of the wet and dry seasons were prefigured in the clear outlines of the distant hills. In the dry atmosphere the decay of vegetation was too rapid for the slow hectic which overtakes an Eastern landscape, or else Nature was too practical for such thin disguises. She merely turned the Hippocratic face to the spectator, with the old diagnosis of Death in her sharp, contracted features.

In the contemplation of such a prospect there was little to excite any but a morbid fancy. There were no clouds in the flinty blue heavens, and the setting of the sun was accompanied with as little ostentation as was consistent with the dryly practical atmosphere. Darkness soon followed, with a rising wind, which increased as the shadows deepened on the plain. The fringe of alder by the watercourse began to loom up as I urged my horse forward. A half-hour's active spurring brought me to a *corral*, and a little beyond a house, so low and broad it seemed at first sight to be half buried in the earth.

My second impression was that it had grown out of the soil, like some monstrous vegetable, its dreary proportions were so in keeping with the vast prospect. There were no recesses along its roughly boarded walls for vagrant and unprofitable shadows to lurk in the daily sunshine. No projection for the wind by night to grow musical over, to wail, whistle, or whisper to; only a long wooden shelf containing a chilly-looking tin basin, and a bar of soap. Its uncurtained windows were red with the sinking sun, as though bloodshot and inflamed from a too long unlidded existence. The tracks of cattle led to its front door, firmly closed against the rattling wind.

To avoid being confounded with this familiar element, I walked to the rear of the house, which was connected with a smaller building by a slight platform. A grizzled, hard-faced old man was standing there, and met my salutation with a look of inquiry, and, without speaking, led the way to the principal room. As I entered, four young men who were reclining by the fire, slightly altered their attitudes of perfect repose, but beyond that betrayed neither curiosity nor interest. A hound started from a dark corner with a growl, but was immediately kicked by the old man into obscurity, and silenced again. I can't tell why, but I instantly received the impression that for a long time the group by the fire had not uttered a word or moved a muscle. Taking a seat, I briefly stated my business.

Was a United States surveyor. Had come on account of the Espíritu Santo Rancho. Wanted to correct the exterior boundaries of township lines, so as to connect with the near exteriors of private grants. There had been some intervention to the old survey by a Mr. Tryan who had pre-empted adjacent — "settled land warrants," interrupted the old man. "Ah, yes! Land Warrants, — and then this was Mr. Tryan?"

I had spoken mechanically, for I was preoccupied in connecting other public lines with private surveys, as I looked in his face. It was certainly a hard face, and reminded me of the singular effect of that mining operation known as "ground sluicing"; the harder lines of underlying character were exposed, and what were once plastic curves and soft outlines were obliterated by some powerful agency.

There was a dryness in his voice not unlike the prevailing atmosphere of the valley, as he launched into an *ex parte* statement of the contest, with a fluency, which, like the wind without, showed frequent and unrestrained expression. He told me — what I had already learned — that the boundary line of the old Spanish grant was a creek, described in the loose phraseology of the *deseño* as beginning in the *valda* or skirt of the hill, its precise location long the subject of litigation. I listened and answered with little interest, for my mind was still distracted by the wind which swept violently by the house, as well as by his odd face, which was again reflected in the resemblance that the silent group by the fire bore toward him. He was still talking, and the wind was yet blowing, when my confused attention was aroused by a remark addressed to the recumbent figures.

" Now, then, which on ye 'll see the stranger up the creek to Altascar's, to-morrow ? "

9 *

There was a general movement of opposition in the group, but no decided answer.

" Kin you go, Kerg ? "

" Who 's to look up stock in Strarberry per-ar-ie ? "

This seemed to imply a negative, and the old man turned to another hopeful, who was pulling the fur from a mangy bear-skin on which he was lying, with an expression as though it were some-body's hair.

" Well, Tom, wot 's to hinder you from goin' ? "

" Mam 's goin' to Brown's store at sun-up, and I s'pose I 've got to pack her and the baby agin."

I think the expression of scorn this unfortunate youth exhibited for the filial duty into which he had been evidently beguiled, was one of the finest things I had ever seen.

" Wise ? "

Wise deigned no verbal reply, but figuratively thrust a worn and patched boot into the discourse. The old man flushed quickly.

" I told ye to get Brown to give you a pair the last time you war down the river."

" Said he would n't without'en order. Said it was like pulling gum-teeth to get the money from you even then."

There was a grim smile at this local hit at the old man's parsimony, and Wise, who was clearly the privileged wit of the family, sank back in hon-orable retirement.

"Well, Joe, ef your boots are new, and you are n't pestered with wimmin and children, p'r'aps you'll go," said Tryan, with a nervous twitching, intended for a smile, about a mouth not remarkably mirthful.

Tom lifted a pair of bushy eyebrows, and said shortly, —

"Got no saddle."

"Wot's gone of your saddle?"

"Kerg, there," — indicating his brother with a look such as Cain might have worn at the sacrifice.

"You lie!" returned Kerg, cheerfully.

Tryan sprang to his feet, seizing the chair, flourishing it around his head and gazing furiously in the hard young faces which fearlessly met his own. But it was only for a moment; his arm soon dropped by his side, and a look of hopeless fatality crossed his face. He allowed me to take the chair from his hand, and I was trying to pacify him by the assurance that I required no guide, when the irrepressible Wise again lifted his voice: —

"Theer's George comin'! why don't ye ask him? He'll go and introduce you to Don Fernandy's darter, too, ef you ain't pertickler."

The laugh which followed this joke, which evidently had some domestic allusion (the general tendency of rural pleasantry), was followed by a light step on the platform, and the young man entered. Seeing a stranger present, he stopped and colored ; made a shy salute and colored again, **and** then, drawing a box from the corner, sat down, his hands clasped lightly together and his very handsome bright blue eyes turned frankly on mine.

Perhaps I was in a condition to receive the romantic impression he made upon me, and I took it upon myself to ask his company as guide, and he cheerfully assented. But some domestic duty called him presently away.

The fire gleamed brightly on the hearth, and, no longer resisting the prevailing influence, I silently watched the spirting flame, listening to the wind which continually shook the tenement. Besides the one chair which had acquired a new importance in my eyes, I presently discovered a crazy table in one corner, with an ink-bottle and pen ; the latter in that greasy state of decomposition peculiar to country taverns and farm-houses. A goodly array of rifles and double-barrelled guns stocked the corner ; half a dozen saddles and blankets lay near, with a mild flavor of the horse about them. Some deer and bear skins completed the inventory. As I sat there, with the silent group around me, the shadowy gloom within and the dominant wind without, I found it difficult to believe I had ever known a different existence. My profession had often led me to wilder scenes, but rarely among those whose unrestrained habits and easy unconsciousness made me feel so lonely and uncomfortable. I shrank closer to myself, not without grave doubts — which I think occur naturally to people in like situations — that this was the general rule of humanity, and I was a solitary and somewhat gratuitous exception.

It was a relief when a laconic announcement of supper by a weak-eyed girl caused a general movement in the family. We walked across the dark platform, which led to another low-ceiled room. Its entire length was occupied by a table, at the farther end of which a weak-eyed woman was already taking her repast, as she, at the same time, gave nourishment to a weak-eyed baby. As the formalities of introduction had been dispensed with, and as she took no notice of me, I was enabled to slip into a seat without discomposing or interrupting her. Tryan extemporized a grace, and the attention of the family became absorbed in bacon, potatoes, and dried apples.

The meal was a sincere one. Gentle gurglings at the upper end of the table often betrayed the presence of the "wellspring of pleasure." The conversation generally referred to the labors of the day, and comparing notes as to the whereabouts of missing stock. Yet the supper was such a vast improvement upon the previous intellectual feast, that when a chance allusion of mine to the business of my visit brought out the elder Tryan, the interest grew quite exciting. I remember he in-

veighed bitterly against the system of ranch-hold-
ing by the "greasers," as he was pleased to term
the native Californians. As the same ideas have
been sometimes advanced under more pretentious
circumstances, they may be worthy of record.

"Look at 'em holdin' the finest grazin' land that
ever lay outer doors? Whar's the papers for it?
Was it grants? Mighty fine grants, — most of
'em made arter the 'Merrikans got possession.
More fools the 'Merrikans for lettin' 'em hold 'em.
Wat paid for 'em? 'Merrikan blood and money.

"Did n't they oughter have suthin out of their
native country? Wot for? Did they ever im-
prove? Got a lot of yaller-skinned diggers, not
so sensible as niggers to look arter stock, and they
a sittin' home and smokin'. With their gold and
silver candlesticks, and missions, and crucifixens,
priests and graven idols, and sich? Them sort
things wurent allowed in Mizzoori."

At the mention of improvements, I involuntarily lifted my eyes, and met the half-laughing,
half-embarrassed look of George. The act did
not escape detection, and I had at once the satisfaction of seeing that the rest of the family had
formed an offensive alliance against us.

"It was agin Nater, and agin God," added
Tryan. "God never intended gold in the rocks to
be made into heathen candlesticks and crucifixens.
That's why he sent 'Merrikins here. Nater never

intended such a climate for lazy lopers. She never gin six months' sunshine to be slept and smoked away."

How long he continued, and with what further illustration I could not say, for I took an early opportunity to escape to the sitting-room. I was soon followed by George, who called me to an open door leading to a smaller room, and pointed to a bed.

" You 'd better sleep there to-night," he said; " you 'll be more comfortable, and I 'll call you early."

I thanked him, and would have asked him several questions which were then troubling me, but he shyly slipped to the door and vanished.

A shadow seemed to fall on the room when he had gone. The " boys " returned, one by one, and shuffled to their old places. A larger log was thrown on the fire, and the huge chimney glowed like a furnace, but it did not seem to melt or subdue a single line of the hard faces that it lit. In half an hour later, the furs which had served as chairs by day undertook the nightly office of mattresses, and each received its owner's full-length figure. Mr. Tryan had not returned, and I missed George. I sat there, until, wakeful and nervous, I saw the fire fall and shadows mount the wall. There was no sound but the rushing of the wind and the snoring of the sleepers. At last, feeling the place insupportable, I seized my hat and, opening the door, ran out briskly into the night.

The acceleration of my torpid pulse in the keen fight with the wind, whose violence was almost equal to that of a tornado, and the familiar faces of the bright stars above me, I felt as a blessed relief. I ran not knowing whither, and when I halted, the square outline of the house was lost in the alder-bushes. An uninterrupted plain stretched before me, like a vast sea beaten flat by the force of the gale. As I kept on I noticed a slight elevation toward the horizon, and presently my progress was impeded by the ascent of an Indian mound. It struck me forcibly as resembling an island in the sea. Its height gave me a better view of the expanding plain. But even here I found no rest. The ridiculous interpretation Tryan had given the climate was somehow sung in my ears, and echoed in my throbbing pulse, as, guided by the star, I sought the house again.

But I felt fresher and more natural as I stepped upon the platform. The door of the lower building was open, and the old man was sitting beside the table, thumbing the leaves of a Bible with a look in his face as though he were hunting up prophecies against the "Greaser." I turned to enter, but my attention was attracted by a blanketed figure lying beside the house, on the platform The broad chest heaving with healthy slumber,

and the open, honest face were familiar. It was
George, who had given up his bed to the stranger
among his people. I was about to wake him, but
he lay so peaceful and quiet, I felt awed and
hushed. And I went to bed with a pleasant impression of his handsome face and tranquil figure
soothing me to sleep.

I was awakened the next morning from a sense
of lulled repose and grateful silence by the cheery
voice of George, who stood beside my bed, ostentatiously twirling a " riata," as if to recall the
duties of the day to my sleep-bewildered eyes. I
looked around me. The wind had been magically
laid, and the sun shone warmly through the windows. A dash of cold water, with an extra chill
on from the tin basin, helped to brighten me. It
was still early, but the family had already break-
fasted and dispersed, and a wagon winding far in
the distance showed that the unfortunate Tom had
already " packed " his relatives away. I felt more
cheerful, — there are few troubles Youth cannot
distance with the start of a good night's rest.
After a substantial breakfast, prepared by George,
in a few moments we were mounted and dashing
down the plain.

We followed the line of alder that defined the
creek, now dry and baked with summer's heat,
but which in winter, George told me, overflowed

its banks. I still retain a vivid impression of that morning's ride, the far-off mountains, like *silhouettes,* against the steel-blue sky, the crisp dry air, and the expanding track before me, animated often by the well-knit figure of George Tryan, musical with jingling spurs, and picturesque with flying " riata." He rode a powerful native roan, wild-eyed, untiring in stride and unbroken in nature. Alas! the curves of beauty were concealed by the cumbrous *machillas* of the Spanish saddle, which levels all equine distinctions. The single rein lay loosely on the cruel bit that can gripe, and, if need be, crush the jaw it controls.

Again the illimitable freedom of the valley rises before me, as we again bear down into sunlit space. Can this be " Chu-Chu," staid and respectable filly of American pedigree, — " Chu-Chu," forgetful of plank-roads and cobble-stones, wild with excitement, twinkling her small white feet beneath me ? George laughs out of a cloud of dust, " Give her her head ; don't you see she likes it ? " and " Chu-Chu " seems to like it, and, whether bitten by native tarantula into native barbarism or emulous of the roan, " blood " asserts itself, and in a moment the peaceful servitude of years is beaten out in the music of her clattering hoofs. The creek widens to a deep gully. We dive into it and up on the opposite side, carrying a moving cloud of impalpable powder with us. Cattle are scattered over the plain, grazing quietly, or banded together in vast restless herds. George makes a wide, indefinite sweep with the " riata," as if to include them all in his *vaquero's* loop, and says, " Ours ! "

" About how many, George ? "

" Don't know."

" How many ? "

" Well, p'r'aps three thousand head," says George, reflecting. " We don't know, takes five men to look 'em up and keep run."

" What are they worth ? "

" About thirty dollars a head."

I make a rapid calculation, and look my astonishment at the laughing George. Perhaps a recollection of the domestic economy of the Tryan household is expressed in that look, for George averts his eye and says, apologetically, —

" I 've tried to get the old man to sell and build, but you know he says it ain't no use to settle down, just yet. We must keep movin'. In fact, he built the shanty for that purpose, lest titles should fall through, and we 'd have to get up and move stakes further down."

Suddenly his quick eye detects some unusual sight in a herd we are passing, and with an exclamation he puts his roan into the centre of the mass. I follow, or rather " Chu-Chu " darts after the roan, and in a few moments we are in the

midst of apparently inextricable horns and hoofs.
" Toro ! " shouts George, with vaquero enthusiasm,
and the band opens a way for the swinging " riata."
I can feel their steaming breaths, and their spume
is cast on " Chu-Chu's " quivering flank.

Wild, devilish-looking beasts are they ; not
such shapes as Jove might have chosen to woo a
goddess, nor such as peacefully range the downs of
Devon, but lean and hungry Cassius-like bovines,
economically got up to meet the exigencies of a
six months' rainless climate, and accustomed to
wrestle with the distracting wind and the blinding dust.

" That 's not our brand," says George ; " they 're
strange stock," and he points to what my scientific
eye recognizes as the astrological sign of Venus
deeply seared in the brown flanks of the bull he is
chasing.   But the herd are closing round us with
low mutterings, and George has again recourse to
the authoritative " Toro," and with swinging " riata "
divides the " bossy bucklers " on either side.   When
we are free, and breathing somewhat more easily, I
venture to ask George if they ever attack any
one.

" Never horsemen, — sometimes footmen.   Not
through rage, you know, but curiosity.   They think
a man and his horse are one, and if they meet a
chap afoot, they run him down and trample him
under hoof, in the pursuit of knowledge.   But,"

adds George, "here's the lower bench of the foothills, and here's Altascar's corral, and that white building you see yonder is the *casa*."

A whitewashed wall enclosed a court containing another adobe building, baked with the solar beams of many summers. Leaving our horses in the charge of a few peons in the courtyard, who were basking lazily in the sun, we entered a low doorway, where a deep shadow and an agreeable coolness fell upon us, as sudden and grateful as a plunge in cool water, from its contrast with the external glare and heat. In the centre of a low-ceiled apartment sat an old man with a black silk handkerchief tied about his head; the few gray hairs that escaped from its folds relieving his gamboge-colored face. The odor of cigarritos was as incense added to the cathedral gloom of the building.

As Señor Altascar rose with well-bred gravity to receive us, George advanced with such a heightened color, and such a blending of tenderness and respect in his manner, that I was touched to the heart by so much devotion in the careless youth. In fact, my eyes were still dazzled by the effect of the outer sunshine, and at first I did not see the white teeth and black eyes of Pepita, who slipped into the corridor as we entered.

It was no pleasant matter to disclose particulars of business which would deprive the old Señor of the greater part of that land we had just ridden over, and I did it with great embarrassment. But he listened calmly, — not a muscle of his dark face stirring, — and the smoke curling placidly from his lips showed his regular respiration. When I had finished, he offered quietly to accompany us to the line of demarcation. George had meanwhile disappeared, but a suspicious conversation in broken Spanish and English, in the corridor, betrayed his vicinity. When he returned again, a little absent-minded, the old man, by far the coolest and most self-possessed of the party, extinguished his black silk cap beneath that stiff, uncomely *sombrero* which all native Californians affect. A *serapa* thrown over his shoulders hinted that he was waiting. Horses are always ready saddled in Spanish ranchos, and in half an hour from the time of our arrival we were again " loping" in the staring sunlight.

But not as cheerfully as before. George and myself were weighed down by restraint, and Altascar was gravely quiet. To break the silence, and by way of a consolatory essay, I hinted to him that there might be further intervention or appeal, but the proffered oil and wine were returned with a careless shrug of the shoulders and a sententious " *Que bueno ?* — Your courts are always just."

The Indian mound of the previous night's discovery was a bearing monument of the new line

and there we halted. We were surprised to find
the old man Tryan waiting us. For the first time
during our interview the old Spaniard seemed
moved, and the blood rose in his yellow cheek.
I was anxious to close the scene, and pointed out
the corner boundaries as clearly as my recollection
served.

"The deputies will be here to-morrow to run
the lines from this initial point, and there will be
no further trouble, I believe, gentlemen."

Señor Altascar had dismounted and was gathering a few tufts of dried grass in his hands. George
and I exchanged glances. He presently arose from
his stooping posture, and, advancing to within a
few paces of Joseph Tryan, said, in a voice broken
with passion, —

"And I, Fernando Jesus Maria Altascar, put
you in possession of my land in the fashion of my
country."

He threw a sod to each of the cardinal points.

"I don't know your courts, your judges, or your
corregidores. Take the *llano !* — and take this
with it. May the drought seize your cattle till
their tongues hang down as long as those of your
lying lawyers ! May it be the curse and torment
of your old age, as you and yours have made it of
mine !"

We stepped between the principal actors in this
scene, which only the passion of Altascar made

tragical, but Tryan, with a humility but ill con-
cealing his triumph, interrupted : —

" Let him curse on.   He 'll find 'em coming home
to him sooner than the cattle he has lost through
his sloth and pride.   The Lord is on the side of
the just, as well as agin all slanderers and re-
vilers."

Altascar but half guessed the meaning of the
Missourian, yet sufficiently to drive from his mind
all but the extravagant power of his native invective.

" Stealer of the Sacrament !   Open not ! — open
not, I say, your lying, Judas lips to me !   Ah !
half-breed, with the soul of a cayote ! — Car-r-r-
ramba !"

With his passion reverberating among the con-
sonants like distant thunder, he laid his hand
upon the mane of his horse as though it had been
the gray locks of his adversary, swung himself
into the saddle and galloped away.

George turned to me : —

" Will you go back with us to-night ?"

I thought of the cheerless walls, the silent figures
by the fire, and the roaring wind, and hesitated.

" Well then, good by."

" Good by, George."

Another wring of the hands, and we parted.   I
had not ridden far, when I turned and looked back.
The wind had risen early that afternoon, and was

already sweeping across the plain. A cloud of dust travelled before it, and a picturesque figure occasionally emerging therefrom was my last indistinct impression of George Tryan.

PART II. — IN THE FLOOD.

THREE months after the survey of the Espíritu Santo Rancho, I was again in the valley of the Sacramento. But a general and terrible visitation had erased the memory of that event as completely as I supposed it had obliterated the boundary monuments I had planted. The great flood of 1861 – 62 was at its height, when, obeying some indefinite yearning, I took my carpet-bag and embarked for the inundated valley.

There was nothing to be seen from the bright cabin windows of the "Golden City" but night deepening over the water. The only sound was the pattering rain, and that had grown monotonous for the past two weeks, and did not disturb the national gravity of my countrymen as they silently sat around the cabin stove. Some on errands of relief to friends and relatives wore anxious faces, and conversed soberly on the one absorbing topic. Others, like myself, attracted by curiosity, listened eagerly to newer details. But

10

with that human disposition to seize upon any circumstance that might give chance event the exaggerated importance of instinct, I was half conscious of something more than curiosity as an impelling motive.

The dripping of rain, the low gurgle of water, and a leaden sky greeted us the next morning as we lay beside the half-submerged levee of Sacramento. Here, however, the novelty of boats to convey us to the hotels was an appeal that was irresistible. I resigned myself to a dripping rubber-cased mariner called "Joe," and, wrapping myself in a shining cloak of the like material, about as suggestive of warmth as court-plaster might have been, took my seat in the stern-sheets of his boat. It was no slight inward struggle to part from the steamer, that to most of the passengers was the only visible connecting link between us and the dry and habitable earth, but we pulled away and entered the city, stemming a rapid current as we shot the levee.

We glided up the long level of K Street, — once a cheerful, busy thoroughfare, now distressing in its silent desolation. The turbid water which seemed to meet the horizon edge before us flowed at right angles in sluggish rivers through the streets. Nature had revenged herself on the local taste by disarraying the regular rectangles by huddling houses on street corners, where they presented abrupt gables to the current, or by capsizing them in compact ruin. Crafts of all kinds were gliding in and out of low-arched doorways. The water was over the top of the fences surrounding well-kept gardens, in the first stories of hotels and private dwellings, trailing its slime on velvet carpets as well as roughly boarded floors. And a silence quite as suggestive as the visible desolation was in the voiceless streets that no longer echoed to carriage-wheel or footfall. The low ripple of water, the occasional splash of oars, or the warning cry of boatmen were the few signs of life and habitation.

With such scenes before my eyes and such sounds in my ears, as I lie lazily in the boat, is mingled the song of my gondolier who sings to the music of his oars. It is not quite as romantic as his brother of the Lido might improvise, but my Yankee "Giuseppe" has the advantage of earnestness and energy, and gives a graphic description of the terrors of the past week and of noble deeds of self-sacrifice and devotion, occasionally pointing out a balcony from which some California Bianca or Laura had been snatched, half clothed and famished. Giuseppe is otherwise peculiar, and refuses the proffered fare, for — am I not a citizen of San Francisco, which was first to respond to the suffering cry of Sacramento? and is not he, Giuseppe, a member of the Howard Society? No!

Giuseppe is poor, but cannot take my money. Still, if I must spend it, there is the Howard Society, and the women and children without food and clothes at the Agricultural Hall.

I thank the generous gondolier, and we go to the Hall, — a dismal, bleak place, ghastly with the memories of last year's opulence and plenty, and here Giuseppe's fare is swelled by the stranger's mite. But here Giuseppe tells me of the "Relief Boat" which leaves for the flooded district in the interior, and here, profiting by the lesson he has taught me, I make the resolve to turn my curiosity to the account of others, and am accepted of those who go forth to succor and help the afflicted. Giuseppe takes charge of my carpet-bag, and does not part from me until I stand on the slippery deck of "Relief Boat No. 3."

An hour later I am in the pilot-house, looking down upon what was once the channel of a peaceful river. But its banks are only defined by tossing tufts of willow washed by the long swell that breaks over a vast inland sea. Stretches of "tule" land fertilized by its once regular channel and dotted by flourishing ranchos are now cleanly erased. The cultivated profile of the old landscape had faded. Dotted lines in symmetrical perspective mark orchards that are buried and chilled in the turbid flood. The roofs of a few farm-houses are visible, and here and there the

smoke curling from chimneys of half-submerged
tenements show an undaunted life within. Cattle
and sheep are gathered on Indian mounds waiting
the fate of their companions whose carcasses drift
by us, or swing in eddies with the wrecks of barns
and out-houses. Wagons are stranded everywhere
where the tide could carry them. As I wipe the
moistened glass, I see nothing but water, pattering
on the deck from the lowering clouds, dashing
against the window, dripping from the willows,
hissing by the wheels, everywhere washing, coil-
ing, sapping, hurrying in rapids, or swelling at last
into deeper and vaster lakes, awful in their suggestive quiet and concealment.

As day fades into night the monotony of this
strange prospect grows oppressive. I seek the
engine-room, and in the company of some of the
few half-drowned sufferers we have already picked
up from temporary rafts, I forget the general
aspect of desolation in their individual misery.
Later we meet the San Francisco packet, and
transfer a number of our passengers. From them
we learn how inward-bound vessels report to having struck the well-defined channel of the Sacramento, fifty miles beyond the bar. There is
a voluntary contribution taken among the generous travellers for the use of our afflicted, and we
part company with a hearty "God speed" on
either side. But our signal-lights are not far dis-

tant before a familiar sound comes back to us, — an indomitable Yankee cheer, — which scatters the gloom.

Our course is altered, and we are steaming over the obliterated banks far in the interior. Once or twice black objects loom up near us, — the wrecks of houses floating by. There is a slight rift in the sky towards the north, and a few bearing stars to guide us over the waste. As we penetrate into shallower water, it is deemed advisable to divide our party into smaller boats, and diverge over the submerged prairie. I borrow a pea-coat of one of the crew, and in that practical disguise am doubtfully permitted to pass into one of the boats. We give way northerly. It is quite dark yet, although the rift of cloud has widened.

It must have been about three o'clock, and we were lying upon our oars in an eddy formed by a clump of cottonwood, and the light of the steamer is a solitary, bright star in the distance, when the silence is broken by the " bow oar" : —

" Light ahead."

All eyes are turned in that direction. In a few seconds a twinkling light appears, shines steadily, and again disappears as if by the shifting position of some black object apparently drifting close upon us.

" Stern, all ; a steamer !"

" Hold hard there ! Steamer be d—d !" is the

reply of the coxswain. "It's a house, and a big one too."

It is a big one, looming in the starlight like a huge fragment of the darkness. The light comes from a single candle, which shines through a window as the great shape swings by. Some recollection is drifting back to me with it, as I listen with beating heart.

"There's some one in it, by Heavens! Give way, boys, — lay her alongside. Handsomely, now! The door's fastened; try the window; no! here's another!"

In another moment we are trampling in the water, which washes the floor to the depth of several inches. It is a large room, at the further end of which an old man is sitting wrapped in a blanket, holding a candle in one hand, and apparently absorbed in the book he holds with the other. I spring toward him with an exclamation: —

"Joseph Tryan!"

He does not move. We gather closer to him, and I lay my hand gently on his shoulder, and say: —

"Look up, old man, look up! Your wife and children, where are they? The boys, — George! Are they here? are they safe?"

He raises his head slowly, and turns his eyes to mine, and we involuntarily recoil before his look.

It is a calm and quiet glance, free from fear, anger, or pain ; but it somehow sends the blood curdling through our veins. He bowed his head over his book again, taking no further notice of us. The men look at me compassionately, and hold their peace. I make one more effort : —

"Joseph Tryan, don't you know me ? the surveyor who surveyed your ranch, — the Espíritu Santo? Look up, old man !"

He shuddered and wrapped himself closer in his blanket. Presently he repeated to himself, "The surveyor who surveyed your ranch, — Espíritu Santo," over and over again, as though it were a lesson he was trying to fix in his memory.

I was turning sadly to the boatmen, when he suddenly caught me fearfully by the hand and said, —

"Hush !"

We were silent.

"Listen !" He puts his arm around my neck and whispers in my ear, " I 'm a *moving off !* "

" Moving off ? "

"Hush ! Don't speak so loud. Moving off. Ah ! wot 's that ? Don't you hear ? — there ! listen !"

We listen, and hear the water gurgle and click beneath the floor.

"It 's them wot he sent ! — Old Altascar sent. They 've been here all night. I heard 'em first in the creek, when they came to tell the old man to move farther off. They came nearer and nearer. They whispered under the door, and I saw their eyes on the step, — their cruel, hard eyes. Ah, why don't they quit ?"

I tell the men to search the room and see if they can find any further traces of the family, while Tryan resumes his old attitude. It is so much like the figure I remember on the breezy night that a superstitious feeling is fast overcoming me. When they have returned, I tell them briefly what I know of him, and the old man murmurs again, —

" Why don't they quit, then ? They have the stock, — all gone — gone, gone for the hides and hoofs," and he groans bitterly.

" There are other boats below us. The shanty cannot have drifted far, and perhaps the family are safe by this time," says the coxswain, hopefully.

We lift the old man up, for he is quite helpless, and carry him to the boat. He is still grasping the Bible in his right hand, though its strengthening grace is blank to his vacant eye, and he cowers in the stern as we pull slowly to the steamer, while a pale gleam in the sky shows the coming day.

I was weary with excitement, and when we reached the steamer, and I had seen Joseph Tryan comfortably bestowed, I wrapped myself in a blanket near the boiler and presently fell asleep. But even then the figure of the old man often started

10 *

o

before me, and a sense of uneasiness about George made a strong undercurrent to my drifting dreams. I was awakened at about eight o'clock in the morning by the engineer, who told me one of the old man's sons had been picked up and was now on board.

"Is it George Tryan?" I ask quickly.

"Don't know; but he's a sweet one, whoever he is," adds the engineer, with a smile at some luscious remembrance. "You'll find him for'ard."

I hurry to the bow of the boat, and find, not George, but the irrepressible Wise, sitting on a coil of rope, a little dirtier and rather more dilapidated than I can remember having seen him.

He is examining, with apparent admiration, some rough, dry clothes that have been put out for his disposal. I cannot help thinking that circumstances have somewhat exalted his usual cheerfulness. He puts me at my ease by at once addressing me : —

"These are high old times, ain't they? I say, what do you reckon 's become o' them thar bound'ry moniments you stuck? Ah!"

The pause which succeeds this outburst is the effect of a spasm of admiration at a pair of high boots, which, by great exertion, he has at last pulled on his feet.

"So you've picked up the ole man in the shanty, clean crazy? He must have been soft to have stuck there instead o' leavin' with the old woman. Did n't know me from Adam ; took me for George !"

At this affecting instance of paternal forgetfulness, Wise was evidently divided between amusement and chagrin. I took advantage of the contending emotions to ask about George.

" Don't know whar he is ! If he 'd tended stock instead of running about the prairie, packin' off wimmin and children, he might have saved suthin. He lost every hoof and hide, I 'll bet a cookey ! Say you," to a passing boatman, " when are you goin' to give us some grub ? I 'm hungry 'nough to skin and eat a hoss. Reckon I 'll turn butcher when things is dried up, and save hides, horns, and taller."

I could not but admire this indomitable energy, which under softer climatic influences might have borne such goodly fruit.

" Have you any idea what you 'll do, Wise ? " I ask.

" Thar ain't much to do now," says the practical young man. " I 'll have to lay over a spell, I reckon, till things comes straight. The land ain't worth much now, and won't be, I dessay, for some time. Wonder whar the ole man 'll drive stakes next."

" I meant as to your father and George, Wise."

" O, the ole man and I 'll go on to ' Miles's, ' whar

Tom packed the old woman and babies last week.
George 'll turn up somewhar atween this and
Altascar's, ef he ain't thar now."

I ask how the Altascars have suffered.

" Well, I reckon he ain't lost much in stock.   I
should n't wonder if George helped him drive 'em
up the foot-hills.   And his ' casa ' 's built too high.
O, thar ain't any water thar, you bet.   Ah," says
Wise, with reflective admiration, " those greasers
ain't the darned fools people thinks 'em.   I 'll bet
thar ain't one swamped out in all 'er Californy."
But the appearance of " grub," cut this rhapsody
short.

" I shall keep on a little farther," I say, " and
try to find George."

Wise stared a moment at this eccentricity until
a new light dawned upon him.

" I don't think you 'll save much.   What 's the
percentage, — workin' on shares, eh ! "

I answer that I am only curious, which I feel
lessens his opinion of me, and with a sadder feeling than his assurance of George's safety might
warrant, I walked away.

From others whom we picked up from time to
time we heard of George's self-sacrificing devotion, with the praises of the many he had helped
and rescued.   But I did not feel disposed to return until I had seen him, and soon prepared myself to take a boat to the lower " valda " of the

foot-hills, and visit Altascar. I soon perfected
my arrangements, bade farewell to Wise, and took
a last look at the old man, who was sitting by the
furnace-fires quite passive and composed. Then
our boat-head swung round, pulled by sturdy and
willing hands.

It was again raining, and a disagreeable wind
had risen. Our course lay nearly west, and we
soon knew by the strong current that we were in
the creek of the Espíritu Santo. From time to
time the wrecks of barns were seen, and we
passed many half-submerged willows hung with
farming implements.

We emerge at last into a broad silent sea. It is
the "llano de Espíritu Santo." As the wind whis-
tles by me, piling the shallower fresh water into
mimic waves, I go back, in fancy, to the long ride
of October over that boundless plain, and recall
the sharp outlines of the distant hills which are
now lost in the lowering clouds. The men are
rowing silently, and I find my mind, released from
its tension, growing benumbed and depressed as
then. The water, too, is getting more shallow as
we leave the banks of the creek, and with my
hand dipped listlessly over the thwarts, I detect
the tops of chimisal, which shows the tide to have
somewhat fallen. There is a black mound, bearing to the north of the line of alder, making an
adverse current, which, as we sweep to the right to

avoid, I recognize.   We pull close alongside and
I call to the men to stop.

There was a stake driven near its summit with
the initials, " L. E. S. I."   Tied half-way down was
a curiously worked "riata."   It was George's.   It
had been cut with some sharp instrument, and the
loose gravelly soil of the mound was deeply dented
with horse's hoofs.   The stake was covered with
horse-hairs.   It was a record, but no clew.

The wind had grown more violent, as we still
fought our way forward, resting and rowing by
turns, and oftener "poling" the shallower surface,
but the old "valda," or bench, is still distant.
My recollection of the old survey enables me to
guess the relative position of the meanderings of
the creek, and an occasional simple professional
experiment to determine the distance gives my
crew the fullest faith in my ability.   Night overtakes us in our impeded progress.   Our condition
looks more dangerous than it really is, but I urge
the men, many of whom are still new in this mode
of navigation, to greater exertion by assurance of
perfect safety and speedy relief ahead.   We go on
in this way until about eight o'clock, and ground
by the willows.   We have a muddy walk for a
few hundred yards before we strike a dry trail,
and simultaneously the white walls of Altascar's
appear like a snow-bank before us.   Lights are
moving in the courtyard ; but otherwise the old
tomb-like repose characterizes the building.

One of the peons recognized me as I entered the court, and Altascar met me on the corridor.

I was too weak to do more than beg his hospitality for the men who had dragged wearily with me. He looked at my hand, which still unconsciously held the broken " riata." I began, wearily, to tell him about George and my fears, but with a gentler courtesy than was even his wont, he gravely laid his hand on my shoulder.

" *Poco a poco* Señor, — not now. You are tired, you have hunger, you have cold. Necessary it is you should have peace."

He took us into a small room and poured out some French cognac, which he gave to the men that had accompanied me. They drank and threw themselves before the fire in the larger room. The repose of the building was intensified that night, and I even fancied that the footsteps on the corridor were lighter and softer. The old Spaniard's habitual gravity was deeper ; we might have been shut out from the world as well as the whistling storm, behind those ancient walls with their time-worn inheritor.

Before I could repeat my inquiry he retired. In a few minutes two smoking dishes of " chupa " with coffee were placed before us, and my men ate ravenously. I drank the coffee, but my excitement and weariness kept down the instincts of hunger.

I was sitting sadly by the fire when he re-entered.

"You have eat?"

I said, "Yes," to please him.

"*Bueno*, eat when you can, — food and appetite are not always."

He said this with that Sancho-like simplicity with which most of his countrymen utter a proverb, as though it were an experience rather than a legend, and, taking the "riata" from the floor, held it almost tenderly before him.

"It was made by me, Señor."

"I kept it as a clew to him, Don Altascar," I said. "If I could find him—"

"He is here."

"Here! and"—but I could not say, "well!" I understood the gravity of the old man's face, the hushed footfalls, the tomb-like repose of the building in an electric flash of consciousness; I held the clew to the broken riata at last. Altascar took my hand, and we crossed the corridor to a sombre apartment. A few tall candles were burning in sconces before the window.

In an alcove there was a deep bed with its counterpane, pillows, and sheets heavily edged with lace, in all that splendid luxury which the humblest of these strange people lavish upon this single item of their household. I stepped beside it and saw George lying, as I had seen him once before, peacefully at rest.   But a greater sacrifice than that he had known was here, and his generous heart was stilled forever.

"He was honest and brave," said the old man, and turned away.

There was another figure in the room ; a heavy shawl drawn over her graceful outline, and her long black hair hiding the hands that buried her downcast face.   I did not seem to notice her, and, retiring presently, left the loving and loved together.

When we were again beside the crackling fire, in the shifting shadows of the great chamber, Altascar told me how he had that morning met the horse of George Tryan swimming on the prairie ; how that, farther on, he found him lying, quite cold and dead, with no marks or bruises on his person ; that he had probably become exhausted in fording the creek, and that he had as probably reached the mound only to die for want of that help he had so freely given to others ; that, as a last act, he had freed his horse.   These incidents were corroborated by many who collected in the great chamber that evening, — women and children, — most of them succored through the devoted energies of him who lay cold and lifeless above.

He was buried in the Indian mound, — the single spot of strange perennial greenness, which the poor aborigines had raised above the dusty plain. A little slab of sandstone with the initials " G. T." is his monument, and one of the bearings of the initial corner of the new survey of tho " Espíritu Santo Rancho."

BOHEMIAN PAPERS.

THE MISSION DOLORES.

THE Mission Dolores is destined to be "The Last Sigh" of the native Californian. When the last "Greaser" shall indolently give way to the bustling Yankee, I can imagine he will, like the Moorish King, ascend one of the Mission hills to take his last lingering look at the hilled city. For a long time he will cling tenaciously to Pacific Street. He will delve in the rocky fastnesses of Telegraph Hill until progress shall remove it. He will haunt Vallejo Street, and those back slums which so vividly typify the degradation of a people; but he will eventually make way for improvement. The Mission will be last to drop from his nerveless fingers.

As I stand here this pleasant afternoon, looking up at the old chapel, — its ragged senility contrasting with the smart spring sunshine, its two gouty pillars with the plaster dropping away like tattered bandages, its rayless windows, its crumbling entrances, the leper spots on its whitewashed wall eating through the dark adobe, — I give the poor old mendicant but a few years longer to sit by the highway and ask alms in the names of the

blessed saints. Already the vicinity is haunted with
the shadow of its dissolution. The shriek of the
locomotive discords with the Angelus bell. An
Episcopal church, of a green Gothic type, with mas-
sive buttresses of Oregon pine, even now mocks its
hoary age with imitation and supplants it with a
sham. Vain, alas ! were those rural accessories, the
nurseries and market-gardens, that once gathered
about its walls and resisted civic encroachment.
They, too, are passing away. Even those queer little adobe buildings with tiled roofs like longitudi-
nal slips of cinnamon, and walled enclosures sa-
credly guarding a few bullock horns and strips of
hide.   I look in vain for the half-reclaimed Mexican, whose respectability stopped at his waist, and
whose red sash under his vest was the utter undo-
ing of his black broadcloth. I miss, too, those
black-haired women, with swaying unstable busts,
whose dresses were always unseasonable in texture
and pattern ; whose wearing of a shawl was a terrible awakening from the poetic dream of the
Spanish mantilla. Traces of another nationality
are visible. The railroad "navvy " has builded his
shanty near the chapel, and smokes his pipe in the
Posada. Gutturals have taken the place of linguals
and sibilants ; I miss the half-chanted, half-drawled
cadences that used to mingle with the cheery " All
aboard " of the stage-driver, in those good old days
when the stages ran hourly to the Mission, and a

trip thither was an excursion. At the very gates
of the temple, in the place of those "who sell
doves for sacrifice," a vender of mechanical
spiders has halted with his unhallowed wares.
Even the old Padre — last type of the Missionary,
and descendant of the good Junipero — I cannot
find to-day; in his stead a light-haired Celt is
reading a lesson from a Vulgate that is wonderfully
replete with double r's. Gentle priest, in thy R-
isons, let the stranger and heretic be remembered.

I open a little gate and enter the Mission Churchyard. There is no change here, though perhaps
the graves lie closer together. A willow-tree,
growing beside the deep, brown wall, has burst
into tufted plumes in the fulness of spring. The
tall grass-blades over each mound show a strange
quickening of the soil below. It is pleasanter
here than on the bleak mountain seaward, where
distracting winds continually bring the strife and
turmoil of the ocean. The Mission hills lovingly
embrace the little cemetery, whose decorative taste
is less ostentatious. The foreign flavor is strong ;
here are never-failing garlands of *immortelles*, with
their sepulchral spicery ; here are little cheap
medallions of pewter, with the adornment of three
black tears, that would look like the three of clubs,
but that the simple humility of the inscription
counterbalances all sense of the ridiculous. Here
are children's graves with guardian angels of great

specific gravity; but here, too, are the little one's toys in a glass case beside them. Here is the average quantity of execrable original verses; but one stanza — over a sailor's grave — is striking, for it expresses a hope of salvation through the "Lord High Admiral Christ"! Over the foreign graves there is a notable lack of scriptural quotation, and an increase, if I may say it, of humanity and tenderness. I cannot help thinking that too many of my countrymen are influenced by a morbid desire to make a practical point of this occasion, and are too apt hastily to crowd a whole life of omission into the culminating act. But when I see the gray *immortelles* crowning a tombstone, I know I shall find the mysteries of the resurrection shown rather in symbols, and only the love taught in His new commandment left for the graphic touch. But "they manage these things better in France."

During my purposeless ramble the sun has been steadily climbing the brown wall of the church, and the air seems to grow cold and raw. The bright green dies out of the grass, and the rich bronze comes down from the wall. The willow-tree seems half inclined to doff its plumes, and wears the dejected air of a broken faith and violated trust. The spice of the *immortelles* mixes with the incense that steals through the open window. Within, the barbaric gilt and crimson look cold and cheap in this searching air; by this light the church certainly is old and ugly. I cannot help wondering whether the old Fathers, if they ever revisit the scene of their former labors, in their larger comprehensions, view with regret the impending change, or mourn over the day when the Mission Dolores shall appropriately come to grief.

JOHN CHINAMAN.

THE expression of the Chinese face in the aggregate is neither cheerful nor happy. In an acquaintance of half a dozen years, I can only recall one or two exceptions to this rule. There is an abiding consciousness of degradation, — a secret pain or self-humiliation visible in the lines of the mouth and eye. Whether it is only a modification of Turkish gravity, or whether it is the dread Valley of the Shadow of the Drug through which they are continually straying, I cannot say. They seldom smile, and their laughter is of such an extraordinary and sardonic nature — so purely a mechanical spasm, quite independent of any mirthful attribute — that to this day I am doubtful whether I ever saw a Chinaman laugh. A theatrical representation by natives, one might think, would have set my mind at ease on this point ; but it did not. Indeed, a new difficulty presented itself, — the impossibility of determining whether the performance was a tragedy or farce. I thought I detected the low comedian in an active youth who turned two somersaults, and knocked everybody down on entering the stage. But, unfortunately, even this classic resemblance to the legitimate farce of our civilization was deceptive. Another brocaded actor, who represented the hero of the play, turned three somersaults, and not only upset my theory and his fellow-actors at the same time, but apparently run a-muck behind the scenes for some time afterward. I looked around at the glinting white teeth to observe the effect of these two palpable hits. They were received with equal acclamation, and apparently equal facial spasms. One or two beheadings which enlivened the play produced the same sardonic effect, and left upon my mind a painful anxiety to know what was the serious business of life in China. It was noticeable, however, that my unrestrained laughter had a discordant effect, and that triangular eyes sometimes turned ominously toward the "Fanqui devil"; but as I retired discreetly before the play was finished, there were no serious results. I have only given the above as an instance of the impossibility of deciding upon the outward and superficial expression of Chinese mirth. Of its inner and deeper existence I have some private doubts. An audience that will view with a serious aspect the hero, after a frightful and agonizing death, get up and quietly walk off the stage, cannot be said to have remarkable perceptions of the ludicrous.

I have often been struck with the delicate plia-bility of the Chinese expression and taste, that might suggest a broader and deeper criticism than is becoming these pages. A Chinaman will adopt the American costume, and wear it with a taste of color and detail that will surpass those "native, and to the manner born." To look at a Chinese slipper, one might imagine it impossible to shape the original foot to anything less cumbrous and roomy, yet a neater-fitting boot than that belong-ing to the Americanized Chinaman is rarely seen on this side of the Continent. When the loose sack or paletot takes the place of his brocade blouse, it is worn with a refinement and grace that might bring a jealous pang to the exquisite of our more refined civilization. Pantaloons fall easily and naturally over legs that have known unlimited freedom and bagginess, and even garrote collars meet correctly around sun-tanned throats. The new expression seldom overflows in gaudy cravats. I will back my Americanized Chinaman against any neophyte of European birth in the choice of that article. While in our own State, the Greaser resists one by one the garments of the Northern invader, and even wears the livery of his conqueror with a wild and buttonless freedom, the China-man, abused and degraded as he is, changes by correctly graded transition to the garments of Christian civilization. There is but one article of

European wear that he avoids. These Bohemian eyes have never yet been pained by the spectacle of a tall hat on the head of an intelligent Chinaman.

My acquaintance with John has been made up of weekly interviews, involving the adjustment of the washing accounts, so that I have not been able to study his character from a social view-point or observe him in the privacy of the domestic circle. I have gathered enough to justify me in believing him to be generally honest, faithful, simple, and painstaking. Of his simplicity let me record an instance where a sad and civil young Chinaman brought me certain shirts with most of the buttons missing and others hanging on delusively by a single thread. In a moment of unguarded irony I informed him that unity would at least have been preserved if the buttons were removed altogether. He smiled sadly and went away. I thought I had hurt his feelings, until the next week when he brought me my shirts with a look of intelligence, and the buttons carefully and totally erased. At another time, to guard against his general disposition to carry off anything as soiled clothes that he thought could hold water, I requested him to always wait until he saw me. Coming home late one evening, I found the household in great consternation, over an immovable Celestial who had remained seated on the front

door-step during the day, sad and submissive, firm
but also patient, and only betraying any animation
or token of his mission when he saw me coming.
This same Chinaman evinced some evidences of
regard for a little girl in the family, who in her
turn reposed such faith in his intellectual qualities
as to present him with a preternaturally uninteresting Sunday-school book, her own property.
This book John made a point of carrying ostentatiously with him in his weekly visits. It appeared usually on the top of the clean clothes,
and was sometimes painfully clasped outside of
the big bundle of soiled linen. Whether John believed he unconsciously imbibed some spiritual
life through its pasteboard cover, as the Prince in
the Arabian Nights imbibed the medicine through
the handle of the mallet, or whether he wished to
exhibit a due sense of gratitude, or whether he
had n't any pockets, I have never been able to
ascertain. In his turn he would sometimes cut
marvellous imitation roses from carrots for his little friend. I am inclined to think that the few
roses strewn in John's path were such scentless
imitations. The thorns only were real. From the
persecutions of the young and old of a certain
class, his life was a torment. I don't know what
was the exact philosophy that Confucius taught,
but it is to be hoped that poor John in his perse-
cution is still able to detect the conscious hate

and fear with which inferiority always regards the possibility of even-handed justice, and which is the key-note to the vulgar clamor about servile and degraded races.

FROM A BACK WINDOW.

I REMEMBER that long ago, as a sanguine and trustful child, I became possessed of a highly colored lithograph, representing a fair Circassian sitting by a window. The price I paid for this work of art may have been extravagant, even in youth's fluctuating slate-pencil currency; but the secret joy I felt in its possession knew no pecuniary equivalent. It was not alone that Nature in Circassia lavished alike upon the cheek of beauty and the vegetable kingdom that most expensive of colors, — Lake; nor was it that the rose which bloomed beside the fair Circassian's window had no visible stem, and was directly grafted upon a marble balcony; but it was because it embodied an idea. That idea was a hinting of my Fate. I felt that somewhere a young and fair Circassian was sitting by a window looking out for me. The idea of resisting such an array of charms and color never occurred to me, and to my honor be it recorded, that during the feverish period of adolescence I never thought of averting my destiny. But as vacation and holiday came and went, and as my picture at first grew blurred, and then faded quite away between the Eastern and Western continents in my atlas, so its charm seemed mysteriously to pass away. When I became convinced that few females, of Circassian or other origin, sat pensively resting their chins on their henna-tinged nails, at their parlor windows, I turned my attention to back windows. Although the fair Circassian has not yet burst upon me with open shutters, some peculiarities not unworthy of note have fallen under my observation. This knowledge has not been gained without sacrifice. I have made myself familiar with back windows and their prospects, in the weak disguise of seeking lodgings, heedless of the suspicious glances of land-ladies and their evident reluctance to show them. I have caught cold by long exposure to draughts. I have become estranged from friends by unconsciously walking to their back windows during a visit, when the weekly linen hung upon the line, or where Miss Fanny (ostensibly indisposed) actually assisted in the laundry, and Master Bobby, in scant attire, disported himself on the area railings. But I have thought of Galileo, and the invariable experience of all seekers and discoverers of truth has sustained me.

Show me the back windows of a man's dwelling, and I will tell you his character. The rear of a house only is sincere. The attitude of deception kept up at the front windows leaves the back area

11 *

defenceless. The world enters at the front door, but nature comes out at the back passage. That glossy, well-brushed individual, who lets himself in with a latch-key at the front door at night, is a very different being from the slipshod wretch who growls of mornings for hot water at the door of the kitchen. The same with Madame, whose contour of figure grows angular, whose face grows pallid, whose hair comes down, and who looks some ten years older through the sincere medium of a back window. No wonder that intimate friends fail to recognize each other in this *dos à dos* position. You may imagine yourself familiar with the silver door-plate and bow-windows of the mansion where dwells your Saccharissa; you may even fancy you recognize her graceful figure between the lace curtains of the upper chamber which you fondly imagine to be hers; but you shall dwell for months in the rear of her dwelling and within whispering distance of her bower, and never know it. You shall see her with a handkerchief tied round her head in confidential discussion with the butcher, and know her not. You shall hear her voice in shrill expostulation with her younger brother, and it shall awaken no familiar response.

I am writing at a back window. As I prefer the warmth of my coal-fire to the foggy freshness of the afternoon breeze that rattles the leafless shrubs in the garden below me, I have my window-

sash closed; consequently, I miss much of the
shrilly altercation that has been going on in the
kitchen of No. 7 just opposite. I have heard fragments of an entertaining style of dialogue usually
known as "chaffing," which has just taken place
between Biddy in No. 9 and the butcher who
brings the dinner. I have been pitying the chilled
aspect of a poor canary, put out to taste the fresh
air, from the window of No. 5. I have been watch-
ing — and envying, I fear — the real enjoyment of
two children raking over an old dust-heap in the
alley, containing the waste and *débris* of all the
back yards in the neighborhood. What a wealth
of soda-water bottles and old iron they have acquired! But I am waiting for an even more familiar prospect from my back window. I know
that later in the afternoon, when the evening paper
comes, a thickset, gray-haired man will appear in
his shirt-sleeves at the back door of No. 9, and,
seating himself on the door-step, begin to read.
He lives in a pretentious house, and I hear he is a
rich man. But there is such humility in his attitude, and such evidence of gratitude at being allowed to sit outside of his own house and read his
paper in his shirt-sleeves, that I can picture his
domestic history pretty clearly. Perhaps he is following some old habit of humbler days. Perhaps
he has entered into an agreement with his wife not
to indulge his disgraceful habit in-doors. He does

not look like a man who could be coaxed into a dressing-gown. In front of his own palatial residence, I know him to be a quiet and respectable middle-aged business-man, but it is from my back window that my heart warms toward him in his shirt-sleeved simplicity. So I sit and watch him in the twilight as he reads gravely, and wonder sometimes, when he looks up, squares his chest, and folds his paper thoughtfully over his knee, whether he does n't fancy he hears the letting down of bars, or the tinkling of bells, as the cows come home and stand lowing for him at the gate.

BOONDER.

I NEVER knew how the subject of this memoir
came to attach himself so closely to the affections of my family. He was not a prepossessing
dog. He was not a dog of even average birth and
breeding. His pedigree was involved in the deep-
est obscurity. He may have had brothers and
sisters, but in the whole range of my canine acquaintance (a pretty extensive one), I never detected any of Boonder's peculiarities in any other
of his species. His body was long, and his fore-
legs and hind-legs were very wide apart, as though
Nature originally intended to put an extra pair between them, but had unwisely allowed herself to
be persuaded out of it. This peculiarity was an-
noying on cold nights, as it always prolonged the
interval of keeping the door open for Boonder's
ingress long enough to allow two or three dogs of
a reasonable length to enter. Boonder's feet were
decided; his toes turned out considerably, and in
repose his favorite attitude was the first position
of dancing. Add to a pair of bright eyes ears
that seemed to belong to some other dog, and a
symmetrically pointed nose that fitted all aper-
tures like a pass-key, and you have Boonder as we
knew him.

I am inclined to think that his popularity was mainly owing to his quiet impudence. His advent in the family was that of an old member, who had been absent for a short time, but had returned to familiar haunts and associations. In a Pythagorean point of view this might have been the case, but I cannot recall any deceased member of the family who was in life partial to bone-burying (though it might be *post mortem* a consistent amusement), and this was Boonder's great weakness. He was at first discovered coiled up on a rug in an upper chamber, and was the least disconcerted of the entire household. From that moment Boonder became one of its recognized members, and privileges, often denied the most intelligent and valuable of his species, were quietly taken by him and submitted to by us. Thus, if he were found coiled up in a clothes-basket, or any article of clothing assumed locomotion on its own account, we only said, "O, it's Boonder," with a feeling of relief that it was nothing worse.

I have spoken of his fondness for bone-burying. It could not be called an economical faculty, for he invariably forgot the locality of his treasure, and covered the garden with purposeless holes ; but although the violets and daisies were not improved by Boonder's gardening, no one ever thought of punishing him. He became a synonyme for Fate ; a Boonder to be grumbled at, to be accepted philosophically, — but never to be averted. But although he was not an intelligent dog, nor an ornamental dog, he possessed some gentlemanly instincts. When he performed his only feat, — begging upon his hind legs (and looking remarkably like a penguin), — ignorant strangers would offer him crackers or cake, which he did n't like, as a reward of merit. Boonder always made a great show of accepting the proffered dainties, and even made hypocritical contortions as if swallowing, but always deposited the morsel when he was unobserved in the first convenient receptacle, — usually the visitor's overshoes.

In matters that did not involve courtesy, Boonder was sincere in his likes and dislikes. He was instinctively opposed to the railroad. When the track was laid through our street, Boonder maintained a defiant attitude toward every rail as it went down, and resisted the cars shortly after to the fullest extent of his lungs. I have a vivid recollection of seeing him, on the day of the trial trip, come down the street in front of the car, barking himself out of all shape, and thrown back several feet by the recoil of each bark. But Boonder was not the only one who has resisted innovations, or has lived to see the innovation prosper and even crush — But I am anticipating. Boonder had previously resisted the gas, but although he spent one whole day in angry altercation with the workmen, — leaving his bones unburied and bleaching in the sun, — somehow the gas went in. The Spring Valley water was likewise unsuccessfully opposed, and the grading of an adjoining lot was for a long time a personal matter between Boonder and the contractor.

These peculiarities seemed to evince some decided character and embody some idea. A prolonged debate in the family upon this topic resulted in an addition to his name, — we called him "Boonder the Conservative," with a faint acknowledgment of his fateful power. But, although Boonder had his own way, his path was not entirely of roses. Thorns sometimes pricked his sensibilities. When certain minor chords were struck on the piano, Boonder was always painfully affected and howled a remonstrance. If he were removed for company's sake to the back yard, at the recurrence of the provocation, he would go his whole length (which was something) to improvise a howl that should reach the performer. But we got accustomed to Boonder, and as we were fond of music the playing went on.

One morning Boonder left the house in good spirits with his regular bone in his mouth, and apparently the usual intention of burying it. The next day he was picked up lifeless on the track, — run over apparently by the first car that went out of the depot.